DAISY CHAIN

Kirstie Malone

To my mum and dad.
I dedicate this, my first novel, to you both. All I
want to do is make you proud.
I love you x

PROLOGUE

Air. Damp. Cold. Molecules of mould clinging to my nostrils, igniting the sickness I'd come to know so well. Like an old friend. Or an enemy.

Head. Thoughts racing. A dull headache. Like a volcanic eruption, ready to cause havoc.

Eyes. Sore. Itchy. Exhaustion clawing at them like a vicious wild animal.

Lips. Cracked. Dehydrated. Painful to touch. Quivering with trepidation.

Breath. Fast. Heavy. Tattooing the frosty air.

Heart. Beating. Pounding. Thumping. Vibrating my tight chest.

Body. An overwhelming sense of nausea. I gag. A lightning bolt of agonising pain. I fall. A vulnerable squeal escapes my lips. A transparent blanket of sickly cold sweat wrapping itself over my fragile frame. Suffocating me.

Hands. Red-raw. Littered with sores. Cut to ribbons by the punishing ground.

Knees. Trembling. Close to my chest. A barrier.

Heat. Thick clouds of pollution, an interlude between icy gusts of wind. Fumes lacing my clothes, encasing my poor body in a musty odour.

Noise. Car horns. Music blaring. Raised voices. Laughter. The soundtrack to London at night. My heart into overdrive.

People. Four hundred to be exact. Not one stopped to talk to me. Zero. Passing one by one or in a group. Some content. Some miserable. None like me. Alone.

Alleyway. Damp. Decaying. Grime seeping through my tatty clothes. Dark. Headlights offering an occasional glimmer of brightness.

Shadow. Creepy. Uninviting. Unfamiliar. Unknown. My blood runs cold, freezing my weak veins. I shake, overcome with terror. Closer and closer. Menacing. Their face becoming clear. Sinister eyes. A cruel smirk.

Fear. Wanting, needing to run but rooted to the spot. My body frail. Shuddering. Tears run down my frost-bitten cheeks, stinging my coarse skin. My tear soaked glare fixated on the figure approaching me.

Closer and closer . . .

Leave me alone . . .

Please don't hurt me . . .

CHAPTER ONE
1996

It was getting late. Lectures had long since finished and no-one was around. Except for one person. Helpless and alone.

The lecture room was fairly plain and boring; the same as the other rooms in this building. It was a place for learning, for bettering yourself, not a tourist attraction. That's what he always said when the students would complain. He wasn't a strict tutor, only raising his voice when he needed to, which was very rare. On the whole, his students were great. Cheeky at times, of course, but they were harmless really.

At night, the room was plunged into darkness, apart from a small trickle of light coming from the moon and the stars that littered the moody sky. You could barely see a thing. It didn't normally matter. People were normally at home or in the bar at this time of day.

Not tonight.

Not Brian Carter.

Lying unconscious on the immaculate sparkling white floor, scarlet blood is seeping from the wound in his head, surrounding his ashen face, staining the collar of his shirt, scruffy and untucked from his trousers.

CHAPTER TWO
Present Day

Like a volcanic eruption,
red hot lava fills our bodies.
It seeps through every vein
and fills every pore of our skin.
Then we begin to shake.
It's uncontrollable.
Every bone in our bodies clashing.
It flares up in a heartbeat
and then it's over before you can even begin
to comprehend,
leaving a trail of devastation in its wake.

*****

Head down, thoughts racing, a dull and constant headache. Like a volcanic eruption, ready to cause havoc. Hair thick with dirt and grease, hanging like curtains in front of an expressionless face. Hands, red-raw and littered with sores, tuck limp strands behind her ears.

Veronica shouldn't be here, not at this party or on this bench. The drops of ice-cold rain, the only reminder of the previous night's thunderstorm, seep through her jeans, stinging her rough, colourless skin. She blinks, her eyes drowning in tears. Murky blue eyes, sore and itchy, exhaustion clawing at them like a vicious wild animal, stare straight ahead at a door, studying every detail, every curve and bend in the wood, every filthy mark that inhabits the surface.

The crimson door is the heart of this community – or at least that's what she assumes from the many bruises littering the dull paint. Just like the human heart it lets people in. Some are respectful of this precious gift; but others abuse the luxury, falling hard against the door, hammering their fists onto it, begging for one more chance. They'll regret it when it's gone. In twenty years, when flats and offices stand in its place, they'll regret treating it so badly. Like a human heart, it can only take so much battering before it gives in completely.

One hundred and four people have passed through that door tonight. She's counted every single one, although she was searching for only four. Three had made their presence known, though not in an obvious way. They hadn't noticed her. Or at least she'd hoped they hadn't. She'd only wanted to check up on them; see they were okay after all these years.

She was fully aware that was all they would ever be to her now: an observation; moving images in her mind. A lot can happen in twenty years. People change. Anything can happen. Everything.

A sharp coldness brings Veronica from her thoughts. The air, damp and cold, laces her tattered, decaying clothes and she slowly brings her knees closer to her chest, desperate for even the tiniest bit of warmth. Desperate for a barrier.

He's moving closer.

Veronica's lips, cracked and sore from dehydration, quiver with trepidation; her breath, fast and heavy, tattooing the frosty air; her heart, pounding, vibrating against her tight chest. Her body is paralysed with fear, causing a transparent blanket of sickly, cold sweat that wraps itself around her fragile frame.

She's terrified of his presence. Terrified of looking into his eyes. Terrified of facing the truth. She wants to run, *needs* to run, but her body is rooted to the spot. Her body is shuddering, nausea rising in her gut, wracked with guilt. She knows she shouldn't feel this way about him. But how could she not? After all that happened.

'I know you.'

*****

Taking a long drag of her cigarette, the nicotine mist painting a layer over her sultry, deep red lips, Karen looks at the woman across the road – or rather she has her eyes firmly set on the man who has just joined her, standing politely at her side, not wanting to startle her. She has no idea why he suddenly felt the urge to go across the road, but it doesn't surprise her. He's probably offering to take her to a nearby shelter or giving her money to make sure she can buy some food. Jason was always too kind for his own good. It's one of the things she loves about him.

Loved.

She flicks her cigarette to the ground, like a small firework against the pavement, and as her spiked Louboutin stubs it out, a cloud of jealousy encases her. It's crazy, she knows, to feel this way about someone so much less fortunate than herself.

Karen has men's attention from the moment she walks into a room; has them fighting for her affections, despite them already being taken by another, whilst that poor woman struggles to even get one person to stop and help. People have crossed the road to be further away from her but have done everything they can to get closer to Karen. Men stare as if she is a Hollywood star and they are adoring fans waiting for a photo or an autograph. Women chat to her as if they have known her all their lives, complimenting her handbag or her jewellery – although that soon changes if their husband or boyfriend is one of those adoring male fans.

Jason's sitting beside the homeless woman now. He's sitting beside this stranger, barely even taking a moment to look over at Karen. She wonders if that woman knows how she is feeling, standing on the opposite side of the road, in a designer dress that shows off her slim figure, glossy dark hair flowing past her shoulders in perfect curls and her make-up mask painted perfectly on her face. She's feeling the one emotion that she really shouldn't, given the situation. Why? Because that woman has got his full attention. Something Karen used to have and something she has yearned after for so many years.

Dropping her gaze down to her diamond wedding band, she sighs.

*****

Jason knows he must tread very carefully. If he is right with his suspicions, this could be a very delicate situation and one he would not want to mess up. He's made enough mistakes to last him a lifetime.

'Someone's birthday, is it?' Veronica asks, her voice hoarse, only just audible.

He follows her gaze to the building across the road. To an outsider, it would look like a happy, long-awaited celebration:

balloons, banners, classic party songs and the loud murmur of excitable voices and laughter. Jason knows differently.

'School reunion. Would have been a laugh if everyone had turned up,' he says, letting out a small groan, feeling like the weight of the world is on his shoulders. Not that he wouldn't be strong enough to take on that weight, with his crisp white shirt stretching over his defined, muscular arms and chest.

'There must be some people here you like . . .' she says, her voice trailing off and for a moment. For a brief moment, Jason is convinced her eyes focus on Karen. But within seconds, she is back to looking down at the ground, as if she is embarrassed at the state she is in. She shouldn't feel that way. Something would have pushed her to this; it wouldn't have been a choice she made.

'A couple. Doesn't really feel the same though. Twenty years is a long time.' Jason sighs before managing to catch Veronica's gaze, looking deep into her eyes, making her squirm. 'But you already know all of this, don't you?'

He waits for her to speak, desperate for her to admit who she really is and tell him why she's here. Not that he's not pleased to see her. He is. Just not in this state. She puts her head down, a deafening silence between the two of them, until Jason gently lifts her chin, the coarseness of her skin cutting against his soft hand.

'Veronica.'

CHAPTER THREE
1997

They'd had so many good nights in this flat, made so many amazing memories, ones they knew would last a lifetime. Today was different. Today the mood was sombre, without a smile or a joke in sight as Veronica stood in front of her friends, trembling, trying her best to hold back her tears. She knew if she let them fall, they'd never stop. She knew if she poured her heart out, she'd never stop.

She'd say too much.

'Do you really have to go?' Karen asked, tearfully.

'Yeah,' Veronica replied, overcome by nausea. She looked as though she'd barely slept, was wearing a pair of tracksuit bottoms and a hoody, without a scrap of make-up on her face.

'But I don't understand . . .' Karen said.

'None of us do,' Jason added.

'You've all said it yourselves – uni has never really suited me. It just got me thinking: what's the point in being here if I don't want to go to lectures?'

'To stay near us?' Karen said. She knew they wouldn't be able to follow each other all the way through life, but at twenty-one, and all of them still acting more immaturely than their years, none of them were really ready to let go just yet.

'Oh come on, this isn't the end. We'll still say in touch.'

'But–' Karen said, devastated at the thought of the group splitting up.

'Karen, please . . . I need to do this. I need a change. I need to get away from this place.'

'Where will you go?' Jason asked.

'I've found myself a little flat. You'll all have to come over for a party when I've settled in properly.'

'You promise?' Jessica asked.

'. . . Yeah,' Veronica replied after some hesitation. She hugged each one of her friends in turn. 'I love you all. Remember that, okay?'

'We love you,' Bradley replied, as Veronica squeezed him tightly.

To him, it all felt very final. Not that he'd break everyone's hearts by telling them that.

CHAPTER FOUR
Present Day

Stubbing out her second cigarette and lighting another, Karen is struggling to contain her jealousy. It's ridiculous, she keeps telling herself. That woman is homeless, living a life on the streets. She's a successful businesswoman with a roof over her head and no money worries. Anyone would choose her life over that woman's. Or would they? *For all the expensive labels and flash cars, my life isn't all it's cracked up to be*, Karen thought, puffing on her cigarette.

She pauses for a moment, realising she's smoked three in as many minutes. He hates her even having one, let alone this many. At least she won't have to disguise the smell when she gets back tonight. She'd normally have to hide the pack in the inside pocket of her handbag, chew minty gum and spray perfume and air freshener to make sure there wasn't even a hint of the tobacco fumes. But he's not home very often, and is away at the moment, has been for the last six weeks. Karen had never known business trips to last so long, to do so much damage to a marriage.

Of course she knows what he's really up to. She isn't a fool. Or maybe she is. Coming to a school reunion on her own. Smoking on her own. Drinking on her own. Standing outside a grotty social club on her own. All because her husband couldn't be bothered to show his face.

She stamps hard on her cigarette, taking her frustrations out on the rain-soaked pavement before looking at Jason again. He tries to put his arm round the woman but she

15

flinches under his touch, making him retract his kindness. Handing her a tissue, he remains fixated on her as she frantically dabs at her eyes. She's probably giving him some sob story about her fall from grace.

Karen feels a pang of guilt for thinking such a horrible thing. The poor woman wouldn't have wanted to be homeless. No-one would. It's not like a career choice or an ambition; you don't aspire to a life on the streets, it just happens. One wrong choice, one bad decision, and you can go spiralling out of control. Who knew this woman's story?

She contemplates joining them across the road. She's not entirely sure if it's to avoid going back into the party, to be closer to Jason, or to help the woman; but whatever her motive, Karen sees them walking in her direction before she can make up her mind. The woman immediately breaks away from Jason when they reach her, shifting from one foot to another. Her feet must be sore, Karen senses, her shoes thin and falling to pieces, with scuff marks on the weather-worn material.

'You waited for me. I'm flattered,' Jason grins, making his way over to Karen.

'I needed a fag,' Karen says, shrugging her shoulders casually, although inside she's cursing herself for looking so desperate.

'Or three,' he says, looking at the cigarette ends littering the ground.

A smirk appears on his face, revelling in her imperfections. It makes him feel like he can rescue her. He's always been that way. Her knight in shining armour.

'I shouldn't have come here tonight. I didn't even want to.'

'So why did you?'

'A moment of madness,' Karen says, letting out a sigh. 'It's made me see that I was just looking back with rose-tinted glasses.'

The whole evening has been a bitter disappointment for Karen, having previously been excited, if not a little nervous, when she had received the Facebook invitation. She'd thought that maybe this was what they'd all been waiting for, the five of them. God knows, she could use a friend.

'Or the same reason as me,' Jason says.

'I didn't even want a reunion. I thought I did, but there's only three of us here, and I'm sorry, but there's no way I can stand being around that cow in there,' Karen says, getting more worked up by the second as she gestures towards the social club.

The real reason for Karen's chain-smoking has been to avoid going back inside where her friend has been propping up the bar with a face like a smacked backside. Friend. Ha! That's a laugh.

'Four,' Jason says, bringing Karen from her thoughts.

'What?'

'There's four of us here.'

Jason goes back into the club and although it's hard, knowing he'll probably be talking to Jessica, Karen keeps her jealousy under wraps, knowing this isn't the time. Jason's movements have revealed the homeless woman, who has spent the last few moments cowering behind him, using his muscular physique as a barrier. Karen looks at her, not knowing what to say. What did he mean by 'four of us'? This woman isn't, wasn't, one of us? She can't be.

Just as Karen is about to question her, the woman lifts her arm, giving her a sheepish little wave. The baggy sleeve of her jacket, at least five sizes too big, rides up her arm, the skinniness of it horrifying Karen. Pale, with a slightly blue tinge, her skin seems pushed to the limit by her bones. Her elbows jut out, almost as if it is independent from the rest of her body.

Her wrist . . .

That's when Karen sees, upon closer inspection, a familiar tattoo. A daisy chain wrapped around her scrawny wrist. Nothing too artistic, it looks more like a small child's attempt at art, and no colour, just a black and white sketched effect. Karen glances down at her own wrist where an identical pattern exists, the monochrome design contrasting with the sun-kissed glow of her skin. She can't fully see it, with part of the tattoo covered by her large sparkly bangle.

Her husband doesn't like it being on show.

This isn't just a homeless woman, it's her former friend. The one she regarded as a sister. The one she cried to in the wake of her father's death. The one she shared a flat with after leaving school. The one she called when things went wrong.

The one who didn't pick up.

Veronica squirms uncomfortably, her eyes flickering as if caught in a dazzling spotlight. She's waiting for Karen to respond, but words are failing her. She can think but she can't speak, and as for breathing . . . right now this natural function has escaped Karen and she feels as though she is being suffocated.

What's happened to her? The tattoo is the only thing that remains of her best friend. The sparkle in her eyes, the sweet but mischievous smile, the flowing locks of golden hair, that infectious laugh . . .

It's all gone.

CHAPTER FIVE
1996

Music was blaring so loudly it made the club vibrate, the beat pulsating in people's bodies. The girls were in the centre of the room, dancing far more childishly than their twenty years. It was always the same on their nights out. The latest tunes playing yet they danced like a bunch of little kids learning a cheesy pop routine. It made them stand out. Although their tiny dresses and killer heels probably helped too.

Veronica leant towards the other girls, whispering something in their ears before leaving the dance floor, in need of a drink, joining Bradley and Jason at the bar.

'Jay, I think you've pulled,' Veronica said to Jason, nudging him.

'Me?' Jason asked, passing her a drink: her usual tipple of double rum and Coke.

'Someone on the dance floor just asked if you were single; referred to you as "the hot guy at the bar".'

'Hot, eh?' Jason grinned cheekily.

'Must have had his beer goggles on,' Karen interrupted, teasing her boyfriend – although she dropped an affectionate kiss on his cheek.

'Oi!' Jason said, gently tickling her sides, making her giggle: they'd been together for three years and had fallen head over heels.

'Don't cry, pretty boy, you know I'm only kidding. You spent more time than me getting ready,' Karen said, turning her attention back to Jason.

'They said to give you this,' Veronica said, handing him a small business card.

Karen peered over Jason's shoulder and struggled to contain her laughter as she read the name on the card: Danny Simpson. With her arms wrapped round Jason she could feel his heart start to thump with dread.

'Please tell me "Danny" is a girl?' Jason asked, worried.

'Oh yeah, sorry, did I forget to mention he thinks you're gay?' Veronica said, amusing them all – apart from Jason who was stood open-mouthed with shock.

'You're joking, right?'

'No,' Veronica replied, her face serious. 'Come on, I couldn't tell him the beautiful brunette on the dance floor is actually your girlfriend, could I?'

'Yeah,' Jason said, getting increasingly wound up, especially as Bradley, his "partner in crime" was shaking beside him, overcome with laughter.

'You could have done a lot worse, Jay. He's cute,' Jess observed, looking over at Danny, who was standing in the middle of the dance floor, waving sweetly at Jason.

'The poor bloke seems besotted, bless him. I couldn't go and break his heart,' Veronica said, shrugging her shoulders casually.

'Veronica!' Jason exclaimed, his cheeks flushing a deep shade of red.

'He said he'll call you in the morning. He knows a great little cafe where you can grab a bite to eat,' Veronica said before turning to Karen. 'You don't mind, do you Kaz?'

'Not at all.' Karen shook her head.

'You're supposed to be sticking up for me,' Jason said, and upon receiving a smile from Karen, he looked at Veronica. 'I can't believe you gave him my number.'

'It's just a bit of fun. You never know, you might get on well,' Veronica said innocently.

'I've got a girlfriend, as you well know. You better go and tell him there's been a mistake,' Jason replied, wrapping a protective arm round Karen, pulling her tightly so she was right beside him.

Suddenly Veronica let out a roar of laughter, unable to contain her amusement for a second longer, prompting the people around them to stare. She had that effect on everyone when she laughed: a dirty, playful giggle that made you smile, even if you'd never met her before.

'It's not funny, Veronica,' Jason said.

'You are so easy to wind up.'

'Excuse me?'

'I'm only m-messing about. Danny's n-not interested in you. He's an old mate of mine, known him for ages, always up for a laugh,' Veronica replied, occasionally stumbling over her words as another ripple of laughter escaped.

'Promise?' Jason asked, holding his breath in anticipation, his nervousness humouring Karen: she's always telling him to watch out for Veronica, the Queen of Pranks. He should know better. After sixteen years of friendship and hundreds of pranks, he should have seen this coming.

'Aww, poor Jay-Jay,' Veronica teased, pulling at his cheeks.

'You really are something else.' Jason shook his head, but he can't help but laugh.

'It's why you all love me,' Veronica said, shrugging her shoulders again.

'That's debatable right now,' Jason replied, taking a swig of his beer.

'That's just made my night. You should've seen your face, mate, it was a picture,' Bradley spluttered, still laughing uncontrollably.

'I don't know what you're laughing at, Brad. I could've sworn I saw him giving you the eye,' Veronica said.

'Seriously?' Bradley asked, his laughter coming to a sudden stop, his face the picture of shock.

'No, course not. Danny's straight, so neither of you are really his type. You guys will believe anything, won't you?' Veronica shook her head in disbelief.

'Should've seen your face, mate, it was a picture,' Jason then said, mocking Bradley.

'So, who's he really interested in?' Jess asked.

'Me,' Veronica smirked, snatching the business card from Jason before turning to wink at Danny.

They watched as Veronica made her way back to the dance floor, joining her potential new love interest, the sea of bodies parting to let her past as if she's royalty. This, like the cheesy dance moves, was a regular occurrence during their nights out. Veronica attracted attention wherever she went and, as the vibrant spotlights highlighted her hair and a youthful twinkle flashed in her eyes, it was clear why.

Karen's best friend was the most beautiful, lively, but loving person she'd ever known. She felt nothing but pride watching her with Danny. It was sure to end in a matter of days, just like every relationship she'd ever had – but that was part of Veronica's charm, part of what made her the person they loved. In many ways, Karen wished she was like her: a crazy whirlwind with a dirty giggle.

But she's not that person anymore.

CHAPTER SIX
Present Day

Karen snaps out of her memories, the sting of tears in her eyes shocking her back to reality, to find Veronica trying to make her escape.

'Wait!' Karen says, catching up with her. It's not hard. In Veronica's condition, she's only managed a few steps. But they were a few steps all the same; a few steps away from Karen.

Veronica looks at her, waiting for her to speak, waiting for reassurance; but Karen can't give it to her. Now up close, all she can see are Veronica's bloodshot eyes, so tired and weepy that Karen swears she can feel her pain. She tries to find some words of comfort for her friend, but the shock has silenced her once again, and Veronica gives up, walking away.

'Veronica, please! I'm sorry, it's just a . . .' Karen catches up with her again, pulling her round by her arm; but she retracts her hand almost instantly, sickened by how malnourished Veronica is.

Before she fully digest what's happening, Karen feels Veronica tug at her arm, plunging her sharp fingernails into her wrist, digging into the perfect daisy chain tattoo, and using the small amount of strength she has left in her body, she pulls Karen closer.

'Leave me alone,' Veronica hisses before walking away for good, leaving Karen in a stunned daze.

*****

Sitting on bar stools beside each other, pop songs blaring from the speakers in the corner of the room, Jessica resides in a comfortable silence with Jason. She would have got the bus straight back home if he hadn't have been here. A night as the victim of Karen's harsh tongue was not the night she had hoped for, but having Jason here has made things a little easier.

'So how have you been?' Jessica asks, breaking the silence between them. Although it isn't the first time they've seen each other this evening, she hasn't previously managed to get his attention long enough other than to exchange the normal pleasantries.

'Could be better,' Jason shrugs, his voice miserable and his eyes full of sadness.

Jessica recognises it. It's the way she sees herself every morning when she looks in the mirror. Fed up. Miserable. Lonely.

'Why?'

'That's a bit forward.'

'Sorry. Blame the wine,' Jessica jokes, raising her half-empty glass.

It works too. He smiles at her. Just a little smile, but a smile all the same. Then, just as quickly as it appears, it fades. It feels strange, being unsure of what to say to one another, how to behave with each other, after all they went through in the past. It's like they're strangers all over again.

'A nasty divorce. Two little boys I never see. And someone I just can't forget.'

'I'm sorry things haven't worked out for you.'

'Trust me, no-one is more sorry than me,' Jason sighs loudly, glancing over Jessica's shoulder as if trying to look through the wall and outside to Karen. Turning back to

Jessica, he flashes her another brief smile. 'Anyway, I'm bored of me. What about you? You met that Mr Right yet?'

'I think I'm past all that.' Jessica shakes her head: if she never goes on another date again it'll be too soon. Especially after last time.

CHAPTER SEVEN
2011

Jessica despised what she saw. Sitting at her dressing table, looking at her reflection in the mirror, she felt ashamed of what she had become. She'd never been the most confident person, but now she never felt more vulnerable. More of a victim.

Glancing at the dress hanging on the back of the bedroom door, tears filled Jessica's eyes. She knew it was a beautiful dress, black and figure-hugging, but it wasn't her. Despite always being quiet and slightly reserved, she'd always dreamt of going out in a bright, eye-catching outfit; one that would make her stand out from the moment she walked into the room; one that would make her feel like someone else.

Like Karen.

Of course, Jessica also knew the reason why Darren, her boyfriend of eight months, had bought this particular dress for her. It was long and it had sleeves. Sleeves to cover the burn marks he had given her a couple of weeks before. Long to cover the bruises on her legs. He'd given her those just two days ago, after he'd come around to see her and found her talking to the postman. Darren had stopped the conversation with one look, and once he and Jessica were inside, he'd kicked her shins, making her fall to the ground as he shouted in her face.

She was his.

*****

Natalie hated him.

Darren was sitting there, making himself at home with a can of beer, a charming smile on his face as he chatted happily to her grandmother. She was like putty in his hands.

Natalie knew different, but her grandmother would never have believed her if she told her, so she kept quiet, her head buried in a book, trying to lose herself in another world. If only it was that easy, she thought, as she was startled by her grandmother's laughter, childishly giggling away at one of Darren's 'jokes'.

It made her angry. She was eight years old and yet she could see through this monster more than her grandmother could. Whoever said that the older you get, the wiser you get?

She was pulled from her thoughts by the sound of her mum walking into the room. Natalie thought she looked beautiful on the outside; but on the inside, she knew her mother would be feeling scared.

'What do you think?' Jessica asked, looking at Darren, trying to work out what sort of mood he was in today. Not that he was likely to kick off. Not in front of her people.

'You look wonderful, darling. Darren's certainly got good taste, choosing such a lovely dress,' her mother said.

'I'm a lucky man. You've got a beautiful daughter,' Darren replied, flashing a grin.

'Bye, sweetheart. Be good for your gran,' Jessica said, making her way over to Natalie and kissing her cheek.

'See ya, kid,' Darren said, ruffling her hair as if she was half her age.

Natalie didn't say another word as Darren wrapped his arm tightly around Jessica's shoulders. She noticed he dug his fingers into the fabric of the dress . . . but before she could say anything, they'd left the flat.

'Shall we put a film on?' her grandmother asked.

'No,' Natalie replied, going into her bedroom, closing the door behind her and putting on her headphones, soothing her worries with the sound of pop music.

CHAPTER EIGHT
Present Day

'You could have your pick of the blokes. You're a good catch.' Jason says, bringing Jessica from her thoughts.

'You think?' Jessica asks, immediately wishing she hadn't responded so enthusiastically. He doesn't love her. Never has. She knows she's making a fool of herself, but the way he smiles at her makes her blush like a love-struck teenager.

'Sure. You're a good person. Funny, kind . . .you can't have changed that much since we last met.'

'Do you think I'm pretty?'

'Yeah, course you're pretty.'

Jessica lowers her head, breaking the eye contact between them. His words affect her more than he will ever know. He probably thinks he's paying her a compliment and that she'll accept it and continue happily with the conversation. Not Jessica. Not after last time.

'Kids?' Jason asks, changing the subject.

'A daughter. Although she's more of a stranger these days,' Jessica tells him, the argument with Natalie weighing heavily on her mind. She tries, she really does, but there's not much of a connection there. It's almost like Natalie hates her, like she's an enemy not her mother. People have told her it's just a phase she's going through. She hopes they're right.

'At least you have her at home with you. That's the main thing.'

'I suppose. Listen, Jase, I need to talk to you.'

'Isn't that what we're doing?' Jason asks, letting out an awkward laugh, once again making Jessica blush slightly.

'Properly talk. In private,' Jessica replies.

Jason gets down from the bar stool. Nerves hit Jessica and her heart starts racing, but before they have the chance to find somewhere quieter, Karen bursts into the room. Jessica watches Jason's face as she heads straight for them. His eyes sparkle, the corners of his mouth twitch, suppressing a beaming smile. Karen doesn't respond, submerged in her own worry.

'She's gone. I can't find her anywhere,' Karen says, breathless with panic.

'Who?' Jessica asks, having been rooted to her bar stool for the last hour, nursing one glass of wine after another.

'What did you say to her?' Jason asks Karen, both of them seemingly oblivious to her presence.

'Nothing. I think that's the problem. I just didn't know what to say. I barely recognised her. But . . .' Karen holds out her arm to Jason, exposing the small but bloody nail marks on her skin.

'Did she do that to you?' Jason asks, horrified.

'Who?' Jessica asks again, more firmly this time. Her whole body burns with irritation. Why can't they just answer her? Why is it that when they're together it's like no-one else exists?

'Veronica,' Jason says quickly, although he doesn't bother to look at her.

'She's here?'

'No, I'm pretty sure I just said she's gone,' Karen snaps, her tongue lashing with sarcasm, as if slapping Jessica round the face. The look on her face tells Jessica she's quite tempted to slap her for real, but for now, she has more on her mind.

'It must have been hard for her, being here tonight. It still doesn't excuse what she did to you though,' Jason says, trying to put a comforting arm around Karen, who steps away from him.

Jessica is stunned by her actions. This was a couple who were in love once, deeply in love, and yet here they are, years later, Karen shrugging him off like a stranger. Mind you, no-one could blame her. Not after what happened. Jessica swallows her guilt with another sip of wine.

'So we just leave her? Let her walk the streets? It's not safe,' Karen says – although it's obvious from her tone of voice that she would be too scared to go out looking for their friend tonight after experiencing her aggression.

'She's been doing it for years. Maybe it's the life she's used to now.'

'She's . . . h-homeless?' Jessica stammers, barely able to form a sentence. Veronica? Homeless? How can she be? She was the life and soul of everything they did. There must be a mistake.

'Obviously. Would it kill you to use your brain for once instead of asking stupid questions?' Karen replies, snapping Jessica out of her thoughts, letting her hostile feelings towards her become crystal clear.

'Karen, stop,' Jason warns her, as if jumping to Jessica's defence. It doesn't last though, as Jason soon softens towards Karen again. 'We'll look for her tomorrow. Give her time to sort her head out. It must be all over the place after tonight, seeing us all again.'

'I'll never forgive myself if something happens to her.'

Jason holds his arms out to Karen, allowing her to fall into his embrace, enveloping her in the safety net of his body.

'I promise she'll be fine, okay? I promise.'

'Jason . . .' Jessica says, desperate to win Jason's attention back, although she knows all her efforts are in vain. He's too wrapped up in Karen to notice or hear anyone else in the room. She gives in, draining the rest of her wine before heading back to the bar to order the same again.

CHAPTER NINE
Present Day

Looking around the room, Bradley struggles to contain his feelings. He feels a wave of tears brewing, although he can't be sure if they have been caused by anger or sadness. He tries to control himself, like always, but the sickly-sweet pink paint on the walls only irritate his eyes further.

Bringing his large but comforting hand to his brown eyes, he wipes the tears from them before turning his attention back to his phone. To the Facebook invite. Class of '95. He wonders what they're doing now. Did they show up to the party? Did Jess, Veronica and Karen bring their husbands? Has Jason found himself a wife? Had they managed to establish good careers, the ones they'd always dreamed of? All he could hope was that his friends were happy, that life had treated them well. He was certain that things couldn't have got any worse.

Jason would find it hilarious if he could see his mate in such a feminine house. A house that barely showed any sign of male presence. Pink walls, spotless white leather sofas, fairy lights draped around the mantelpiece. It's not Bradley's idea of a warm, cosy place to live, somewhere he can switch off after a busy day at the hospital, but anything for a quiet life.

As if on cue, the living room door opens and a sheepish-looking woman – long blonde hair pulled into a ponytail, no make-up on, a tired and withdrawn complexion – walks into the room. His wife. Danielle. Bradley glances at her, his heart breaking at the sight of her. She looked incredible on their wedding day six years ago, like she'd just stepped out of a bridal magazine. Her hair styled and her make-up subtle but still highlighting his favourite part of her: her eyes. She was glowing that day. Of course, he still thought she was beautiful, but the glow she'd had on their wedding day had died.

Bradley offers Danielle a weak smile as she shuffles over to him. She sits beside him on the sofa, takes the mobile phone from his lap and looks at the Facebook invite.

'Go,' Danielle says.

'It's too late.' Bradley shakes his head. The invite says 7pm until late and it was only just coming up for 9pm now, but he could guarantee that Danielle would change her mind and call him home before he was even halfway down the road.

'I know you don't really want to be here. You've been moping around all night,' Danielle says, sighing heavily. 'When you've *actually* been here.'

'I was working until six, you know that,' Bradley replies.

'Were you?' Danielle asks, narrowing her eyes in suspicion.

'Do you want food on the table? A roof over your head? Nice clothes to wear?' Bradley asks, frustrated by Danielle's immaturity, receiving a gentle nod from his wife. 'Then I have to work. Money doesn't grow on trees.'

'I wish it did. All our problems would be solved.'

'Just like that,' Bradley says, his words fuelled with sarcasm.

'Do you know what, just go. Go on. Either go to work or to the party. Do whatever you want but don't hang around here if you're just going to upset me. I'm really fragile right now.'

Bradley wouldn't mind, but she's not just fragile today. She's fragile every day. Clock-watching, calling him in panic if he's so much as five minutes late, checking his phone and pockets after a night out. He knows deep down it's not her fault, she's been through a lot; but so has he, and he wanted more from marriage than a string of blazing rows and accusations flying back and forth.

He watches Danielle bite her lip, tugging gently at a strand of her hair. It's what she always does when she feels guilty, so Bradley relents and takes her hand.

'I haven't done anything wrong, Danielle. I gave up the chance to see my friends again so I could be here with you. The moment I got your text I told the cab driver to turn around and bring me here. I'd say I'm a pretty good husband for doing that.'

'Yeah . . .you're right. I'm sorry,' Danielle says quietly. 'Please go to the party. I'll feel bad if you don't.'

'It's fine. You need me here.'

*****

Danielle doesn't feel comforted by Bradley's words. She knows he'd rather be at the party, having a few beers, letting his hair down. He's been working today. *All day.* And his friends meant a lot to him. She's sure they still do. He talks about them all the time.

Veronica was the life and soul of the party; a chatterbox who barely stopped for breath; a personality that captured everyone in the room within seconds. Karen was the glamorous one – or at least as glamorous as a uni student on a tight budget could be. Jessica was the quietest of the group, Bradley had told her. A beautiful girl but constantly in Veronica and Karen's shadows, lacking in self-confidence no matter how much they all tried to build her up.

Then there was Jason. Bradley talked about him the most. His closest friend in the world back then. His brother. Danielle's unsure how she feels about Jason; he sounds like he was a player back then. In a way, it makes her happy that Bradley is no longer in contact with him; that way he can't be led astray.

Her eyes cast over to the framed wedding photo on the mantelpiece, and the glow of the fairy lights glisten against the diamante detailing of the frame. Perfection. That's what she thought that day. He was perfect. She looked perfect for him. They were perfect together.

She looks at him now, sitting beside her, looking straight ahead, his mind elsewhere and she wonders if she still makes him happy.

CHAPTER TEN
Present Day

The mind is a complex thing,
Too complex for even the smartest to understand.
Years of misery and anger building up,
but a body can only take so much abuse, whether
it be mental or physical.
Maybe it's voices.
Lots of voices all speaking at the same time,
getting louder and louder,
until the only thing that will stop them,
the only thing that will allow you peace and
quiet,
is to release that anger.

*****

Life used to be so good. She'd give anything to go back in time.

She used to be so strong. She'd give anything to be that strong again.

Not that Veronica has anything to give, except a lifetime of hating herself. Hating what she'd done. She'd contemplated telling the truth so many times. She'd searched the phonebook, searched the internet, picked up the phone . . .but she couldn't go through with it. She couldn't bear to give all the details, re-live it all over again.

Not face to face anyway. It would tear Veronica apart to speak of what happened. See them crumble in front of her eyes, tears streaming down their faces. So instead she kept quiet. You think she chose the coward's way out?

You'd be right.

Veronica stumbles on the kerb as she embarks on the next section of the pavement. Her feet can't take much more, almost as shattered as her body. She drags her feet as if she's lost all feeling, patches of red-raw skin showing through the tattered shoes she wears. Just ahead of her, she can see two people. One girl, one boy, can't be any older than eighteen. They glare at her with complete disgust and she wishes she'd never made eye contact with them.

'Look at the state of that!' the teenage girl shouts as they walk towards Veronica.

'Jog on, love, your type gives this place a bad reputation,' the boy warns, a threatening look on his face.

Veronica tries to pass them without causing any more trouble, but they follow her, pulling her back by her collar, almost choking her. They are no more than an inch from her, staring into her eyes with revulsion.

'She's a junkie. Look at her eyes. She's gagging for another fix,' the boy says, letting go of Veronica's jacket with such aggression he almost knocks her off her feet. Bumping against the wall, she tries to stay as far from the youths as she possibly can. Her eyes flick down to the pack of cigarettes in the girl's hand and then back to her, watching as she takes a long drag of the one she has just lit.

'What? You want one of these?' the girl asks.

The young girl walks towards Veronica and before she can stop her, she lifts the sleeve of her jacket, pressing the cigarette hard into Veronica's abused skin. It sizzles against her arm, forming an excruciating scorch mark.

Veronica yelps like an abandoned puppy, but the girl pushes the cigarette even harder, seemingly enjoying watching her suffer. The pain is unbearable, is stealing the breath from her lungs. Tears burn her eyes and she grits her teeth as she desperately tries to free her wounded arm.

The girl lets go of Veronica, thrusting the cigarette to the ground. The reek of burnt flesh rises to her nostrils. She gags.

'Go get your own!' the girl snarls.

'Tramp,' the boy hisses, standing beside her, a couple of wild animals sizing up their prey.

The boy then pushes her to the ground, shoving her so hard that as her back crashes against the pavement, she feels like it might actually be broken. The teens obviously think the same as they rush down the road, glancing over their shoulders several times to make sure no-one is trying to chase them down. They needn't worry. No-one would dare stick up for someone like Veronica.

Lifting herself slowly from the ground, a crippling pain soars through every fibre of her being, forcing a loud groan to escape her lips. Shuffling towards the kerb, she perches for a while, trying to calm herself, the sound of her breathing filling her ears, muting the normal Saturday night murmur. Taking short, sharp breaths, she feels on the verge of a panic attack. This is normal for her. Once a fun, vibrant, carefree woman, she now experiences panic attacks on a daily basis and, in an attempt to take control, she slows her breathing down, closes her weary eyes, trying to count each breath steadily in her head.

A car races past, startling her out of her almost-calm state, sending her heart pounding out of her chest. She's shaking. Her hands. Her legs. Her feet. Like a shattering earthquake, each bone in her body shakes with so much force she's frightened they'll smash into each other and break, leaving her as nothing more than a pile of skin on the side of the road, ghostly white flesh littered with purple and yellow bruises.

Veronica wonders, *would anyone care*? Maybe someone would take pity on her, want to put her back together again. Or maybe they'd simply look away, keep driving, barely giving her a second of their time, as if she were roadkill.

The second option is far more likely.

CHAPTER ELEVEN
Present Day

Some time has passed since Karen burst into the club, worrying herself into a frenzy over Veronica. After taking her to one side and talking things through with her, Jason managed to give her the reassurance she needed and she ordered another drink.

Jason's watching her now, although he can't be sure it's really her. The real Karen. She always enjoyed a night out, but never like this. He knows she's just trying to drown her sorrows. It can't be easy for her, being in his and Jessica's company after so many years, especially after the way they parted.

It doesn't stop Jason feeling jealous though. Karen's with some blokes now. Apparently, they were in their year at uni, but Jason can't remember them. She's sat on one of the guy's laps, flirting outrageously, laughing at everything they say. Jason bangs his fist on the bar, overcome with envy, catching Karen's attention. She strides over to him, amused by his bad mood.

'What's up, grumpy?' Karen asks, leaning on the bar.

'Making a show of yourself, aren't you?' Jason says, glaring over Karen's shoulder at the sleazy blokes still ogling her.

'It's called having a laugh. You should try it sometime.'

'Flirting with a load of strangers isn't my idea of fun.'

'Could've fooled me,' Karen says, bluntly.

Jason doesn't say anything, fails to form a worthy response. She's telling the truth and Jason can't blame her for that. It still hurts though. He watches her look at Jessica, who has witnessed Karen's behaviour but has said nothing, a frown firmly etched on her face.

'Laugher lines are a lot more attractive than frown lines, you know?' Karen snaps at Jessica, who again doesn't respond. Jason knows she's hurt by her friend's criticism.

'You never used to be like this,' Jason says.

'What, so I used to be boring?'

'No. You just never used to be so . . .wild. Out of control.'

'Some men find it sexy,' Karen says, winking at the blokes sitting at her table.

'Those guys certainly do,' Jason mutters, finding it hard to keep calm when all he really wants to do is punch the living daylights out of them for daring to leer at his girl. *His* girl.

She'll always be his girl.

'Jealous?' Karen asks, turning her attention back to him.

'Insanely,' Jason replies, looking at her until she responds, gazing deeply into his eyes.

'Come and sit down with us, Karen,' Jessica says, interrupting their moment, and Jason isn't sure if she's done it on purpose.

'Why?'

'It'll be nice to catch up. I've hardly seen you tonight,' Jessica says.

'That was the plan,' Karen replies sarcastically.

'Behave,' Jason warns Karen, growing a little tired of having to keep the peace between the two women.

'You look lovely,' Jessica says, turning her attention to Karen, although all she gets in return is a moody eye-roll from her estranged friend.

'It's been good to see you, Jess,' Jason says, nudging Karen. 'Hasn't it?'

Karen doesn't reply; instead, she sips her wine, turning her attention yet again back to the nameless blokes she's become acquainted with.

'And you look great,' Jason reassures Jess, not wanting her to feel any worse than she probably already does.

'So do you. If I'm honest, I wasn't sure if I should come tonight.'

'We're really glad you did. Aren't we, Karen?' Jason says, nudging her again.

'Ecstatic,' Karen replies mockingly, her words stinging Jess.

Karen finishes her drink, holding up her glass to a passing barman.

'Same again, darlin',' Karen says, speaking to him in a much friendlier manner than she had Jess.

'Jason . . .' Jessica says.

'Maybe you should slow down a bit,' Jason says to Karen, concerned for her. He's aware he's cut Jess off, but right now, Karen is his priority. Karen will always be his priority.

'Maybe you should mind your own business,' Karen snaps back.

'Jason, I need to speak to you,' Jessica says, more forceful than before.

'You know, desperation really isn't attractive, Jess. Just a little tip for you,' Karen bites back at her, forcing Jess to leave the club, unable to take any more of her cruelty.

'Well done. That's two of our friends that have done a runner. You going to try and get rid of me next?' Jason asks, sighing. This was certainly not the night he had hoped it would be.

'I don't think I could even if I tried,' Karen replies, and Jason watches as a smile appears on her face.

Finally, for the first time that night it feels as though he has her undivided attention.

*****

Making her way home, walking cautiously down the passageway beside the block of flats she resides in, a group of kids, probably around primary school age, ride past Jessica on their bikes. It's far too late for children of their age to be out, especially in an area like this. Even Jessica feels uneasy walking by herself, and after some of the things she's witnessed, nothing should really bother her anymore. The kids circle around her, like they so often do, and one of them even spits on the path in front of her, his saliva bubbling on the uneven surface.

Vile.

She raises her head, determined to walk with confidence, show them she's not someone they should mess around with. She almost loses her footing as she reaches the steps, but manages to grab the railing just in time, the coldness biting at the palm of her hand. The kids laugh. Of course they do. A woman nearly falling over is the funniest thing in the world.

Not.

Climbing the steps to her flat proves a little challenging: they are laced with a fresh frost. It must be heading into minus temperatures tonight. It seems fitting really, the weather matching the atmosphere at the party. Frosty. Cold. Icy. And that was just Karen.

Jessica lets herself and the room starts to spin. She's not drunk. She never gets drunk. Just tipsy. Stepping further into the flat, Jessica wishes she'd made an exception tonight. The living room, her living room, is a mess. Empty beer cans and pizza boxes litter the table and floor, a cold slice of pizza staining the rug with its orangey-red grease. A vase from the side table lies on the carpet, a chunk of ceramic missing, and

Jessica's sure there is an odour of cigarette smoke in the air.

Natalie, her fourteen-year-old daughter, is slouched on the sofa, sipping a can of beer, completely ignoring her mother's presence.

'What the hell have you done?' Jessica asks, in disbelief and horror, immediately feeling her blood start to boil. *Stay calm, Jess, stay calm.*

'Had a party.' Natalie shrugs her shoulders casually.

'Did I give you permission?' Jessica asks.

'You weren't here,' Natalie replies, taking another sip of her beer before Jessica snatches it from her.

'No. I was out. Trying to have fun for once.'

'You were at a party. I thought I'd have one of my own.'

'You're fourteen.'

It's so difficult to cope with Natalie's behaviour at times. Jessica often thinks back to when she was fourteen years old herself and how she was so much better behaved. She had her moments, of course she did, but on the whole, she was a good girl.

Not Natalie. Some days it's like she's the reincarnation of the devil.

'And?' Natalie asks.

'And you shouldn't be drinking. Look at the state of this place!' Jessica shouts.

'I did ask to come to your party but you said no. You've only got yourself to blame for this,' Natalie says.

'The invite said no kids allowed,' Jessica replies – although deep down she knows it's a lie. She hadn't wanted her there, ruining what was supposed to be a happy occasion with her sulky face and sarcastic comments.

'I saw it on Facebook. It said everyone was welcome. I can read, you know.'

'I'm surprised, seeing as you spend more time bunking off than you do in the classroom.'

'Shut up, Mum. Just because your party was crap, don't go taking it out on me,' Natalie says, huffing and puffing like she's hard done by – one of the many traits Jessica finds infuriating.

'I grounded you yesterday,' Jessica reminds her, feeling like she's stuck on repeat, saying the same things to her daughter over and over again.

'And?'

'Grounded means no going out, no skipping school, and certainly no parties.'

'So, you basically want to keep me prisoner?'

'Don't be so bloody dramatic! You could have watched TV or done your homework.'

'Homework's for losers.'

'I wonder if you'll still think that when you're flipping burgers for a living!' Jessica screams, letting her anger take over. Her daughter really knows how to push her buttons. She shouldn't retaliate, she knows that, but Natalie makes it so difficult.

'Oh, chill out!' Natalie groans, switching on the TV, turning the volume up loud.

Jessica gives up and goes into the kitchen . . . to be greeted with the disgusting sight of today's dirty dishes and used coffee mugs piled up on the kitchen counter, one on top of the other, looking as though they'll topple over any second. Jessica marches out of the room, the ghastly smell of leftover food lingering in the air.

'I thought I told you to wash those dishes?' Jessica says, her frustration rising once again.

'Why can't you do it?' Natalie asks, barely looking away from the TV screen.

'Because I'm not the only one living here. It's about time you started pulling your weight.'

'I'm going out.' Natalie gets up from the sofa, making her way towards the front door.

Jessica steps in front of her, blocking her path. She'd let Natalie storm off before, not to be seen for the next twelve hours, only coming back when she'd run out of money – or because she was hungry.

Not this time.

' It's late,' Jessica says.

'It's half ten. You're so pathetic, coming home from a party this early,' Natalie says, laughing at her mother, trying to dodge past and get to the door. Her attitude angers Jessica more than anything else. She doesn't deserve to be laughed at, especially not by her child. It's humiliating.

Jessica grabs her arm, pulling her away from the door.

'Ow! Get off!' Natalie shouts, trying to wrestle herself free from Jessica's grip.

'Give me your key,' Jessica says sternly, refusing to let go.

'How will I get back in?'

'You won't, because you're not going out.'

Natalie glares her Jessica before reluctantly handing over her key. Jessica loosens her hold on her daughter's arm and, almost immediately, she starts making her way towards the door again.

'If you step out of that front door, I'm not letting you back in and it's a very cold night out there,' Jessica warns her. She knows it probably sounds harsh, but it's only because she knows Natalie is about to back down. She's full of empty threats and, after months of bad behaviour, Jessica knows every trick in the book.

'Mum!' Natalie complains, stamping her feet like a child in the middle of a temper tantrum.

'Go to your room. Now!' Jessica shouts, her voice loud and booming, eyes firmly locked with Natalie, letting her know she isn't going to back down.

Natalie finally gives in, grabbing her phone and some leftover pizza and storming off into her bedroom. Jessica waits patiently: 3 . . . 2 . . . 1 . . .

SLAM!

*****

The taxi stops outside Jason's bar and he turns to Karen, who is sitting across from him, having left the middle seat empty. She lends him a warm smile, but she says nothing as he climbs out of the taxi, passing the driver his fare. Searching his pockets as he heads towards his front door, Jason's alarmed to find them empty except for his phone. No wallet. No keys.

Rushing back to the taxi, before the driver has chance to pull away, Jason opens the passenger door.

'I can't find my keys!' Jason says.

'Check your pockets again,' Karen replies.

'I have,' Jason says, flashing her a grin. 'Don't suppose I can stay at yours, can I?'

'I don't think that's a good idea.' Karen shakes her head, folding her arms across her chest. She's become a pro in putting up her guard. It breaks Jason's heart to know he's the root cause of this, but now he's with her again, he's determined to put things right.

'I'll sleep on the floor if it'll make you feel better.'

'Jason . . .'

'Please? I'll be on my best behaviour.'

'You can stay, but you have to leave first thing in the morning.'

'Whatever you want.'

Jason climbs into the taxi, except this time he slides over to the middle seat, wanting to be as close to Karen as he possibly can. She seems a little uneasy as the taxi pulls away from the kerb, but Jason places a friendly kiss on her cheek and suddenly he feels her relax in his company.

CHAPTER TWELVE
Present Day

*I feel so stupid, writing things down in
such an artistic way,
as if that will make a difference.
I haven't done this to hurt you; you've
been through more
than enough.
I'm just trying to sort things in my
head and let you into my thoughts so
that, maybe, you'll realise that I feel
exactly the same as you.
Heartbroken.
Angry.
And pain like you would not believe.
I may as well slap you in the face for
all the help this letter will be though.
It'll be a lot less patronising and
painful.
It'll be over quicker.
I'm going to a lot of trouble to connect
with you but I realise having read this
letter a million times that the only
thing I should be saying,
need to be
saying, is—*

Veronica is in a housing estate, sitting on a bench opposite a row of houses. She watches as a taxi pulls up outside one of the houses, and a couple of lads in their early twenties climb out carrying a pack of beers and a couple of takeaway pizza boxes. She looks at the beer and food, in awe of it, clutching her stomach, experiencing severe hunger pains.

One of the lads catches sight of Veronica, causing her to go into a panic. She gets up from the bench, ignoring her pain and walks away, as quickly as possible.

The two lads go into the house, without giving Veronica another thought.

'Sorry,' Veronica whispers as she hobbles along the pavement and into the night.

CHAPTER THIRTEEN
Present Day

Stepping out of the lift and following Karen towards her home, Jason feels himself grinning. A huge grin that makes his face ache. He can't remember the last time he smiled this way. Perhaps it was when they were last together. It must be. Everything fell apart the day she left. No-one has ever made him feel the way she did.

Reaching the front door, he watches Karen as she takes a deep breath, preparing herself to go inside – not the normal reaction to arriving home after a long day. After composing herself, she unlocks the door and lets Jason inside.

'Wow! Look at this place!' Jason gasps, amazed by the beautiful setting before him: a gorgeous penthouse apartment, like something straight out of a glossy magazine. It's his idea of heaven. Floor-to-ceiling windows and ultra-modern black and white decor throughout, he feels like he's in Hollywood, not London.

'It's alright,' Karen shrugs, immediately removing her shoes. Jason doesn't know a lot about fashion but he can tell they're designer. Karen doesn't seem to care though, casting them aside like an old pair of slippers.

'*Alright*? Sweetheart, I'd give anything to live in a place like this,' Jason says, rushing over to the window, taking in the breath-taking view of the city: seeing it like this, it looks like the most magical place in the world. 'Look at this view.'

'It gets boring after a while,' Karen sighs.

The open plan layout of the apartment means Jason notices as soon as Karen goes into the kitchen, opening the fridge like she's on a mission. Taking out a bottle of wine, she pours herself a large glass before holding up the bottle, offering Jason a drink. He nods before turning his attention back to the living room. It's the type of place he's always dreamt of living in. All the mod cons . . . in fact some of them aren't even mod cons, they look like stuff from the future.

'This TV is huge. You should see mine. It's an embarrassment compared to this,' Jason says, staring up at the large television hanging on the wall: it must be at least a sixty-inch plasma.

'It's too big for this room,' Karen says, passing Jason the glass of wine. Their fingers touch for a second before she snatches her hand away.

'This room is bigger than my whole flat.'

'Sounds good to me. Cosy,' Karen responds, shocking Jason with her honesty. Surely anyone would be happy with a lifestyle like this? He certainly would be.

'A cramped flat above a bar, or a swanky penthouse apartment? I know which I'd choose,' Jason says.

'Maybe we're not as alike as we first thought.'

'I'd love to live here. With you,' Jason replies, edging closer to Karen, wishing he could take her hand, hold her like he did at the party, show her how much she means to him, even after all these years.

'Don't,' she warns him, putting her hands up in defence.

'I can't help how I feel.'

'We're not teenagers anymore and, in case you've forgotten, I'm married,' Karen says, pointing to her wedding ring, a huge sparkly diamond, the kind that's impossible to miss.

'I noticed the ring. I just presumed it was a fashion accessory,' he says.

Karen bows her head, avoiding Jason's gaze. They both know what he means. She's a stunning woman and she has men throwing themselves at her wherever she goes. Or at least Jason imagines she does. She always did when they were younger. But she always remained classy, something that was very rare of the girls in their year. Karen wouldn't go out with just anyone, they had to be special. She thought he was special once.

'The way you were acting tonight. You were all over those guys at the party,' Jason says. If he's honest, he was shocked to his very core. Flirting and kissing other men with her wedding band firmly in place. Karen's not like that, never has been.

'You're one to talk about being faithful,' Karen reminds him, getting defensive.

'My mistakes are the exact reason I'm saying this. I've cheated in the past. I know I have. But was it worth it? Did it make me happy? No. And if I could I'd change it all. In a heartbeat.'

'I was only having fun. Or trying to. It's not like I dragged any of them back here, is it?'

'You might have done if I'd left you to it. God knows what kind of state you'd have been in if I hadn't been there.'

'Give it up, Jase. You're not my knight in shining armour, and you never will be, so you can stop trying. I was flirting and said some things to those guys I didn't mean, but it was the drink talking, not me. You, on the other hand–'

'You're lonely, aren't you?' Jason asks, interrupting her. He doesn't want to be reminded of what he did.

Again, she drops eye contact, squirming uncomfortably on the spot. 'No.'

'Is that him?' Jason asks, nodding his head in the direction of a photograph of Karen with a smartly dressed, smug-looking bloke. She is so out of his league, it's unreal.

'My husband? Yeah,' Karen says, although she doesn't bother looking at the photo.

'You could do better than him. So much better.' Jason shakes his head, looking at the photograph again. Karen all dolled up looking gorgeous and him, the husband, a gluttonous grin on his face and a sleazy glint in his eye, his arm wrapped firmly round Karen's waist. The sight makes Jason's blood boil.

'Alright I get it, you don't approve. You want me to leave him,' Karen snaps and Jason knows he's touched a nerve. 'Is that what all this is about? Pretending you've lost your keys so you can have your wicked way with me?'

'The red light's been flashing on the answer machine since we walked through the door. Calling to cancel plans, was he? Was he supposed to come to the reunion tonight? My guess is that it's not the first time he's let you down.'

'Enough! Okay? Just stop! What makes you think you can start giving me lectures on my marriage? I haven't seen you for twenty years. You have no right to judge me!'

'I just want you to be happy.'

'And you think getting back with you is what will make me happy?'

'I never said anything about us getting back together,' Jason replies, his stomach flipping with optimism . . . maybe she's thought about him just as much as he's thought about her over the years.

'It's what you meant though, wasn't it?' Karen says, flushing with humiliation.

'Was it?' Jason asks, feeling a smirk creep onto his lips.

'Don't start playing games with me, Jason. We grew out of them a long time ago,' she warns, glaring at him . . . and he can't help but wonder if this is because she's angry with him or because she's embarrassed by what she's said.

*****

Lying in bed, trying to bury himself in the safety of his duvet, Bradley keeps his eyes firmly shut. His mind is whirring, replaying old memories as if stored on old rolls of film. Birthdays. Christmas. School trips. Holidays. Concerts. Nights out. Heart to hearts. They did it all, the five of them, barely leaving each other's sides in the whole seventeen years of friendship they shared.

He hears Danielle enter the bedroom, immediately shattering the tranquillity of his thoughts.

'Bradley . . .' she whispers, climbing into bed.

Bradley ignores her, keeping his eyes firmly closed, although he's not sure why he even bothers because she keeps talking anyway. She always does. It's like she knows he's pretending as soon as she walks in the room. Bradley feels her hand rest gently on his shoulder, the only part of his body, except his head, that isn't covered, and he opens his eyes a little. It makes a nice change to feel her affection instead of the wrath of her insecurities.

'I'm sorry,' Danielle says, apologising for the third time this evening. Or maybe it's the fourth. She says it so often these days Bradley loses count.

'It's okay,' he says, closing his eyes again, hoping she'll let him drift off to sleep. He already knows how tomorrow will begin: she'll be even more "fragile" than she was today, and that means Bradley needs all the strength he can get.

'I shouldn't have shouted at you like that. I know how important your friends were to you, you talk about them often enough,' she replies.

Bradley turns over so he's facing his wife, realising she isn't going to relent. Little chats before sleep is one of her habits. Annoying habits. He used to love staying up late with her, talking, laughing, getting to know each other; but nowadays he works twelve to fourteen hours at the hospital, and when he comes home he just wants to relax. Just for one night Bradley would love to come home to a nice meal with his wife, settle down with a film and go to bed feeling happy and stress-free. No falling out with each other, no awkward silences.

'I should have let you go,' Danielle says, obviously still feeling guilty.

'Life goes on. I'll get over it.'

'Are you angry with me?' she asks.

'Of course not. It's been a tough day for everyone, that's all,' Bradley lies, too exhausted for another row.

'It'll be even worse tomorrow. You will be there, won't you?' she asks, just like she has every day for the last two weeks. It happens this time every year without fail. Bradley would understand if he was the kind of bloke that let people down, but he's not. He knows what she's been through. He doesn't want to cause her any more pain.

'Yes. I told you I would be.'

'I love you,' she whispers, turning off her beside lamp.

Bradley doesn't respond. Not that he doesn't love her, because he does. Despite her flaws he loves her more than he ever thought possible to love another human being. But he's angry with her for making him miss the party.

He's been thinking about the others all night. Did they all turn up? How are they? Did they swap numbers? Will they see each other again? Closing his eyes, hoping to fall into a peaceful sleep, he makes a promise to himself that he'll track them down.

*****

Sitting beside Karen on the sofa, Jason's never felt happier. They used to do this all the time when they were together. Looking into each other's eyes, talking and laughing over a bottle of wine or a couple of cans of beer. Sometimes even just a cup of coffee. It didn't matter where they were or what they did, as long as they were with each other, nothing else mattered.

'Do you remember when we first got together?' Jason asks.

'How could I forget? You made me feel like a princess,' she replies, and for the first time since coming home, she smiles softly.

'That's what you were to me. You always will be,' he tells her, meaning every single word. There have been other women in his life, but no-one will ever compare to his first love.

Karen looks at Jason as if hypnotised by his words, her mind probably replaying events of twenty years ago as if they're being shown on an old-school projector. Jason leans forward, making his intentions clear . . . but she immediately backs away, getting up from the sofa.

'I'm going to go and get changed if that's okay?' Karen says.

'Sure, it's your home,' Jason says, although he can't deny his frustration.

'Help yourself to whatever's in the fridge. I won't be long.'

She makes her way into the bedroom, leaving Jason alone with his thoughts for a few moments before poking her head round the door.

'There are some pillows and blankets in the spare room,' she says.

'I can still stay?'

'Only on the sofa. Paul will go mad if knows someone's slept in the spare bedroom,' Karen tells Jason, sounding a little frightened of her husband.

Glaring at his smug face on the photograph again, his body filling with rage, Jason wishes Paul was here right now so he could tell him how lucky he is to have a woman like Karen, how much he wishes she was in love with him instead.

'Is there anything that pleases him?' Jason asks, looking back at Karen.

'Money,' she replies, shrugging her shoulders in discontent.

'I'd live in a cardboard box without a single penny to my name if it meant I had you,' Jason says.

Karen gives him a look, warning him to stop talking before she closes the bedroom door again. Jason knows he shouldn't have said it, it's too soon, but he doesn't get the impression Paul showers her with love. Karen deserves a compliment from time to time, but Paul's kicked her down so much she doesn't feel worthy of kind words.

*****

Standing against the bedroom door, Karen's eyes cast over the bedside tables. One for him. One for her. On his side lie a pair of silver cufflinks and a smart tie. He didn't put them there, nor did he ask Karen to, but she likes to do it. It makes her feel like she's not alone. Like he's just gone for a shower.

On Karen's side, it's a different story. A glass of water and sleeping pills. They never move from the table. She needs them. Without the pills, she will lie awake all night wondering what Paul's doing, who he's with. She gets so wound up that she gives herself a headache. The pills make things easier. For a night, anyway. They lie beside a packet of cigarettes and a lighter.

She must remember to hide them. If he were to return unexpectedly and find them, he'll fly into a rage. It's happened before. That was when she promised to quit. But she can't. She likes smoking, likes the taste of the nicotine and the smell that hangs in the air for a while. It probably sounds disgusting, but living like this, in such a sterile, unwelcoming place, it's nice to do something rebellious every now and then. Karen likes that. It's a part of her.

Tonight she feels she can be herself for the first time in a while. Jason doesn't mind if she says something stupid or if she leaves things lying around. He lets her be herself, something that should feel normal but these days is more of a luxury.

It's comforting to have someone around the place. Normally she sits alone on the sofa, drowning in the leather, watching rubbish on the stupidly massive TV. She told him not to buy it, to get some modest, tasteful furniture, but what Paul wants, Paul gets. Never mind the fact he's hardly ever here.

Karen can't believe Jason actually had to ask if she remembers them getting together. It was the best day of her life – apart from the day the five of them met. He made her feel so special, like he'd lay down his whole life for her. Nothing was ever too much trouble, as long as it made her happy. *If only every man would do the same, us women would be far more content with life*, Karen thinks to herself.

Opening the drawer in the bedside table she takes out a photograph. It's one of those photos that brings back memories as soon as you look at it; makes you smile and feel warm inside. Glowing, even.

CHAPTER FOURTEEN
Summer 1993

It was the summer of 1993. After sharing a picnic, the girls decided to sunbathe on the field, lying side by side, relishing the sizzling heat. The boys were talking amongst themselves, taking a little respite under a tree.

'Sooo, is Jason theee one?' Veronica asked, her words a little slurred as she resided in a deep state of relaxation.

'I know it's still quite new but I really think he might be,' Karen told her. She'd only been with Jason for a year but it felt right. He wasn't just her boyfriend. He was the type of man her father would have been proud of, and that was what mattered to her.

'And you're the one telling me to slow down,' Veronica joked. She was right. Karen was constantly telling her to take her time with relationships instead of falling for the first guy that showed her a bit of attention. That year she'd been with a string of blokes: David, Will, Billy, Jake . . . Karen had lost count after Jake. It wasn't that Veronica was an easy target, she just wanted to be loved.

'It's only because I care.'

'Yeah, I know. I'm really happy for you.'

'Really? It's not too weird for you two, is it?' Karen asked. The five of them had been friends for years, since the first day of school in fact, and then suddenly two of them had got together.

'I thought it would be, but you've changed so much since being with him,' Veronica reassured her.

'In a good way?'

'*A very good way,*' Jess added, joining the conversation. She was the youngest and definitely the quietest of the three girls.

'You went crazy after losing your dad and that's understandable. I mean none of us blamed you, but it felt like we were going to lose you,' Veronica said.

Karen went through a really hard time after her dad passed away. She was thirteen and she found him dead on the living room floor after school one day. No warning. No illnesses in the past. That was it. Dead at forty. Heart attack.

The next couple of years were a downward spiral for Karen: bad behaviour, parties, exclusion from school. Then, sat on Brighton beach one weekend when they were seventeen, Jason declared his love for her and everything changed.

'I never knew you felt that way,' Karen said, stunned by Veronica's revelation.

'We did, but then you fell for Jason.'

'He saved you,' Jess said, and Karen could hear the smile in her voice.

Karen propped herself up using her elbows, lifting her sunglasses onto the top of her head, resting them in her raven hair. She looked over at Jason, smiling sweetly at him. He winked back, making her heart flutter with pleasure.

'Wow! You really have fallen hard, haven't you?' Veronica teased, nudging Karen.

'Maybe,' Karen smirked, laying back down.

'If the way you two look at each other isn't love then I really don't know what is.'

'You're so lucky, Kaz,' Jess sighed. Unlike Karen and Veronica, Jess had remained single throughout school.

'I didn't know you fancied Jason,' Karen said.

'No, no, I didn't mean that. I just meant you're lucky to have someone who loves you.'

'You'll find someone, Jess, but it'll be difficult.'

'Why?' she asked, a frown etched on her face.

'Because you're the baby of the group. We need to inspect each boy very, very carefully. We won't have you go out with just anyone,' Veronica explained.

'That's sweet,' Jess smiled.

'It's our job to look after you,' Veronica said, reaching out her arm to Jess and pulling her in for a quick hug.

'But don't worry, someone will come along eventually. Someone as pretty as you won't be single for long,' Karen said, wanting to build her friend's confidence.

'Promise?' Jess asked.

'Cross my heart. And believe me, it's so worth the wait when that special guy comes along,' Karen told her, unable to take the beaming smile from her lips.

'Yeah alright, Juliet,' Veronica laughed.

Suddenly the boys rushed towards over, shaking cans of Coke and spraying the contents at the girls, soaking them and making them jump to their feet. They liked to give as good as they got back then, and Veronica grabbed some leftover food and threw it at Bradley, starting a food fight. They couldn't stop laughing as they chased one another around the field, the thrill of being in each other's company taking their breath away.

Bradley caught Jess, tickling her, making her laugh harder, before Veronica jumped on his back sending them crashing down to the grass. Jason grabbed Karen, pulling her close to his bare chest, kissing her passionately.

Bradley ushered everyone into a group, his Instamac camera in his hand. 'Everyone get in!'

They huddled together as he held the camera up in the air, all trying to squeeze into the photograph.

'CHEESE!'

Snap!

Another precious memory captured, ready to show their future children and grandchildren as they sit comfortably in their rocking chairs in an old folk's home. That was the way they thought their lives would go. If only they'd known then what they knew now . . . would their smiles have been quite so wide and bright?

CHAPTER FIFTEEN
Present Day

Karen looks at the photo one last time, taking in their beaming smiles. They'd laughed so much that day. The kind of laughter that makes your stomach hurt and your cheeks ache. She hasn't done that in years.

Locking the photo safely back in the drawer, Karen goes into the bathroom to change.

*****

Jason can't deny that as he's sitting here, still reclining in the comfort of the sofa, that he's imagining he's Paul. That he's the one with the stylish apartment and the gorgeous wife. Then something suddenly occurs to him: Karen has no children. Jason always thought she'd go on to be a brilliant mother, so loving and fun. Maybe Paul didn't want any. Maybe Karen's scars run too deep.

*****

Wearing a silk dressing gown and her hair in a messy bun, her "war paint" removed for the night, Karen goes back into the living room. She's been gone for some time but Jason doesn't seem to mind. He looks right at home on the sofa, clearly deep in thought. She startles him with her presence and he hurries to pour her another glass of wine.

'Thank you,' Karen says, accepting his offering before sitting beside him on the sofa.

'You know, I never understood how you always look so beautiful,' he tells her, turning so they are facing each other.

'Oh, don't. I haven't got a scrap of make-up on,' Karen says, brushing off his compliment. She feels her cheeks tingle with the inevitable rosy blush and she wish that she'd kept her foundation on.

'You don't need it,' he replies.

'Full of compliments tonight, aren't you?'

Jason doesn't reply this time. He is staring instead, looking completely in awe of her.

'Have I got something on my face?' she asks, feeling a little self-conscious in his gaze. Despite her lifestyle, she's never been one who likes to be the centre of attention. Except when she's drunk.

'Yeah. Just here.' He kisses her cheek softly. 'And here.' He kisses her other cheek just as gently as the first, his eyes closed, lost in the moment.

Karen feels his lips move further down her face, planting tender kisses along her jaw line, so soft, so gentle, as if she's the most important, most special thing in his world. The tenderness of his lips ignites a feeling she thought had been lost forever: exhilaration. Paul never makes her feel like this.

And happy. *I haven't felt true happiness in a very long time.*

And love. *I've never stopped loving him.*

'That's so cheesy,' Karen giggles, her racing heart pumping excitement through her veins in the same way it pumps her blood.

'Are you complaining?' he asks, pulling away. Despite slating her husband, she can tell he doesn't want to cause trouble for anyone. He's a good man. Always has been.

Her first love.

Their eyes lock. She's missed his eyes. Her arms snake round his neck, pulling him close, his breath on her skin, laced with wine. Her hands move to his chest. The frantic beating of their hearts matching each another, Jason leans in closer, like he did earlier that evening, but this time Karen find herself responding. Their lips crash together, their actions fuelled by a cocktail of lust and wine, and suddenly it's like they are those two love-struck seventeen-year-olds again.

CHAPTER SIXTEEN
Present Day

She comes here every year. The same day, the same time, once a year. Or at least she thinks she does. Having spent so long on the streets, Veronica seems to have lost all sense of time. Days roll into nights and back into days again. The sun turns to wind and rain and then into snow and back to sun again. It's a blur, most of the time.

A stray tear falls, stinging her cheek, adding a little moisture to her otherwise dehydrated skin, and she wipes it away, anger bubbling inside her. She mustn't cry. She doesn't deserve to. There's a fresh bed of floral tributes in front of the charcoal-grey headstone, each with their own little card attached. Reading each note of condolence, a lump forms in the back of Veronica's throat. So much love and loss in one place. So many people grieving for the same person. Still grieving after all this time.

She wonders how many people would grieve for her.

Running a finger along the name engraved into the stone, a shiver races down her spine, making her shudder, despite the stormy night having given way to a calm, mild morning. He should still be here, walking the streets, living his life. Instead, people have to come and stand by a block of stone in the ground to remember him. She often wonders what he'd be like now, what his life would be like. Would he be retired? Would he spend his days with grandchildren? Or would he have moved away with his wife, be residing in a peaceful little cottage by the sea?

Veronica hates being here. The way it brings back memories. Bad memories. She never plans to come. It's like an involuntary movement. She finds herself dragging her poor body to this graveyard, year in, year out . . .

Quiet mumbled voices and gentle footsteps in the distance bring her from her thoughts and she realises her time is up. A stolen moment to pay her respects is all she gets. It's all she deserves to have. In fact, it's far more than she deserves. As the sound of the nearby family gets a little louder, indicating they are fast approaching, Veronica pulls herself up from the ground, a soaring pain taking over every bone in her body as she finds the nearest gate. Shuffling along the grass, shoulders hunched, head down, she prays they won't see her.

CHAPTER SEVENTEEN
Present Day

Jessica hears Natalie leave her bedroom. It's eight in the morning and she'd never normally be up at this time, but she's recently got a Saturday job at a clothes shop in town. She didn't do it off her own back. Jessica asked around, put in a good word, got her the interview. She even had to go with her to make sure she actually turned up. Natalie's hated it from day one, choosing to bunk off and hide in the flat all day. She gets away with it, too, given the hours Jessica works, but today is a rare day off.

Jessica has just finished a phone call, her mobile still in her hand, and she's sure Natalie has only come into the room to be nosey and muscle in on her private life.

'Who were you talking to?' Natalie asks, appearing behind her mother. Lurking more like. Lurking like the devil.

'A friend,' Jessica says, shoving her phone into her pocket.

'One of them from the reunion?'

'Why do you care?'

'Only trying to make conversation,' Natalie says, shrugging her shoulders. It's an irritating habit of hers. One of many.

'Get going or you'll miss the bus,' Jessica says, knowing exactly what is going through Natalie's mind, much to the young girl's horror.

'I'm not going in.' She shrugs. Again.

'It's only a few hours.'

'It's like eight whole hours. It's the weekend. I should be relaxing.'

'I think you do enough relaxing at school.'

'I don't.'

'Your teacher called me the other day to say you were asleep in her lesson,' Jessica says, raising her eyebrows.

Jessica is forever getting phone calls at work from teachers complaining about Natalie's behaviour. It infuriates her. How can she possibly get her work done when she has to sort all of her daughter's problems too?

'Shouldn't be so boring then, should she?'

'I'm not arguing about it anymore.'

'Why aren't you in work?'

'It's my day off. I did tell you I was off today.'

'Two days off in a row and you call me lazy,' Natalie says, tutting, as if she's telling her mother off. As if she's the parent. She does it a lot and Jessica can't stand it. People talking down to her. Especially when those people are her family. People that are supposed to care.

'I think anyone would agree that what I do is a lot harder than what you do.'

'I need my keys back,' Natalie says, holding out her hand expectantly.

'No chance. I'll be here all day so I can let you in,' Jessica tells her, narrowing her eyes. It always worked when she was little. Any time she did something wrong, Jessica would give her this glare and she'd give up trying to fight with her.

Mind you, Natalie wasn't always a bad girl.

'Mum! You're so annoying!'

Jessica offers Natalie a smile, wanting to try and put things right before her shift, but she glares back at her, giving her "evils" as Natalie would say. Then it happens.

The same thing that happens almost every Saturday, or at least the Saturday's Jessica is at home.

Natalie gets up from her seat, causing it to fall to the ground, grabs her coat and leaves the flat.

SLAM!

*****

As Jason opens his eyes, he finds himself staring at the large chandelier hanging from the ceiling. Confused, he scans the room, taking in his surroundings through his blurred, tired vision.

'I thought I told you to let yourself out,' Karen says, indicating her presence, and Jason immediately turns to face her. Even first thing in the morning she looks stunningly beautiful. Stood in the doorway of her bedroom, already dressed in her designer gear, she looks like she's stepped straight off the catwalk.

'And where would I have gone?' Jason asks, trying to focus his mind.

'Not my problem,' Karen shrugs. He knows she pretends not to care but they definitely had a moment last night. He's sure of it. It felt like old times . . . until she stormed out of the room.

'I've lost my keys, remember? Did you really want me to sleep rough for the night?' Jason asks, trying to catch her gaze.

'You can go now. I'm sure one of your staff will be there to let you in,' Karen says.

'I was thinking we could spend some time together actually,' Jason says, keen to get back in her good books. He never liked it when she was in a mood.

'Didn't you get the message last night?' Karen asks.

'Not really, no. One minute you're having a go at me, the next you're kissing me, and then just when I think you've forgiven me, you go cold and push me away,' Jason says, feeling himself getting increasingly worked up. Perhaps he was wrong for getting his hopes up. Thing is, he knows she feels the same.

'It's complicated,' Karen says, her eyes casting over to the answer machine in the corner of the room. The red light flashes, still illuminating their vision, making it impossible to ignore.

'He's cheating on you,' Jason tells her.

'You know nothing about me and Paul,' Karen says.

'Last night told me a lot about you and Paul.'

'And suddenly you're an expert on love and marriage.'

'I know he doesn't treat you right. He goes on long *business trips* and comes home with lipstick on the collar of his shirts,' Jason says, and he can tell he's touched a nerve as she bows her head. 'I know I'd treat you so much better than he does.'

'Let me take you back to the summer of 1997 . . .'

'The summer I made the biggest mistake of my life.'

CHAPTER EIGHTEEN
1997

Jason was in bed, the double bed he shared with Karen . . . only he wasn't with her. He was holding Jessica in his arms as they looked into each other's eyes. Jessica seemed a bit uncomfortable under his gaze. She wasn't used to getting attention, having always been the quietest in the group. The other girls were particularly protective of her.

She looked gorgeous to Jason, even though her make-up was a little smudged and her hair a mess. He leant in to kiss her but she moved her head slightly.

'We shouldn't be doing this,' Jessica said, exhaling, her voice shaking, perhaps with excitement; but Jason suspected it was more down to fear.

'You wanted this as much as I did,' Jason reminded her, possibly to shift the blame from himself.

'What about Karen?' Jess asked, and he had to admit he felt a pang of guilt for his long-term girlfriend . . . but his lust for Jess was too strong to ignore.

'Walk away if that's what you really want. I won't stop you,'

Jessica hesitated for a moment before leaning in to kiss Jason, making his heart race.

SLAM!

Jason heard the front door to the flat close loudly, but before he even had a chance to pull away from Jessica, Karen opened the bedroom door, freezing in horror at the sight before her.

'Karen!' Jason exclaimed, horrified at being caught.

'It's not how it looks. Please, Karen, it was a mistake!' Jess said, pleading with her friend; but it was in vain as she stormed out of the room. 'Karen!'

Jessica got out of bed, and dressed herself as quickly as possible in complete silence. Leaping out of bed with his back to Jessica, Jason pulled his t-shirt on. His heart pounding, his mouth dry, a sickening sense of nausea brewing in the pit of his stomach.

Jason was shaking so much that as he stepped into his jeans, his hands couldn't stay still long enough to fasten the zip and button. He gave up, rushing out of the bedroom, through the flat and out into the corridor.

Karen was leaning against the wall, a little distance from the flat, her hands behind her back, as if to steady her shell-shocked body. Bradley was at her side trying to get her to speak, but she was unable to find the words to form an audible response. He took his eyes off Karen and looked in Jason's direction, taking in both his and Jess's bedraggled appearances, his jaw literally dropping.

'Please don't tell me this is what I think it is,' Bradley said, looking at the two of them, horrified. 'You didn't?'

'They did,' Karen said, without bothering to look at them, her voice cracking with emotion.

'How could you? Look at the state of her. Make you feel good, does it? Knowing you've broken her heart? She's supposed to be your best friend, Jess!' Bradley said, furious with their behaviour.

'I never meant for this to happen,' Jess said.

'And you!' Bradley turned to Jason, as if spitting venom. 'You're supposed to love her.'

'I do love her,' Jason said, turning his attention to his girlfriend, desperate for her forgiveness. 'Karen, I do. Please can we talk about this.'

'Do you really think she wants to talk to you after what you've done?' Bradley said. Jason normally loved his protective nature, it was one of the best qualities you could ask for in a friend, but he was growing tired of his interference right now.

'Five minutes,' Jason pleaded, looking at Karen to avoid Bradley's angry glare.

'Leave her alone,' Bradley said.

'No offence, Brad, but stay out of this. This is between me and Karen,' Jason said, cursing him for trying to ruin his chances to reconcile with her.

'You've got two minutes,' Karen said.

'Thank you,' Jason replied, offering her a kind smile, although it didn't work in his favour, as Karen shot him a furious stare.

'But I don't want anything more to do with you,' Karen said to Jess.

'I'm sorry,' Jess told her, devastated as tears spilled down her cheeks. 'Please just let me–'

'I don't want to hear it,' Karen said coldly, shaking her head.

Jessica made her way down the corridor, trying to make eye contact with Bradley as she passed, but he completely blanked her. Jason was heartbroken. Their friendship was admired by so many and now, in the space of just a few moments, it had all come tumbling down around them. Because of him. Jason would never forgive himself.

'You should dump him, not hear his pathetic excuses,' Bradley said to Karen, confused by her decision.

'There's something he needs to know,' Karen replied.

CHAPTER NINETEEN
Present Day

Jason watches Karen push the food around her plate. He's cooked her a full English, despite it being her home and not his, and he's worried about her sudden change in mood. The colour has drained from her face; her attitude is weary. Life has been hard on her and now they've been reunited, Jason feels it's his duty to take care of her. Despite it being twenty years since his betrayal, he still hasn't forgiven himself.

'It'll do your hangover the world of good,' he says, although he senses it's more than just alcohol that's caused her headache.

'I can't eat,' Karen says.

Jason wonders if it's because of today's meaning – the anniversary of Mr Carter's death – but with the red light still flashing on the answer machine, he suspects it's more to do with her husband. He can't help but feel for her.

'Do you want something else? Cereal? Toast?' Jason offers.

'You don't have to play host. This is my home,' Karen says, letting the fork fall from her hand so it clatters against her plate.

'Sorry,' Jason says, not wanting to cause her any more upset.

'No, it's okay. I've got a lot on my mind right now. It's nothing personal . . . well, maybe a bit personal,' Karen says, looking at him, the corners of her mouth forming the faint image of a smirk.

'Why do you put up with it?'

'He's my husband. I made vows on my wedding day that I intend to keep.'

'But you still flirted with those guys last night. And you kissed me.'

'That wasn't the real me. It was just the drink,' Karen repeats.

'Do you love him?' Jason asks; just the very idea of Karen being in love with another man makes his heart ache.

'For richer, for poorer, in sickness and in health . . .' Karen says, avoiding his gaze.

'That's a no then.'

'I never said that.'

'When people say their vows, nowhere does it say you have to put up with being cheated on by your husband. In fact, the church frowns upon adultery.'

'I'm not religious.'

'Neither am I, but I still know it's wrong. I know I'm the last person you want to hear this from but you deserve so much more,' Jason tells her. He tries to take her hand but she snatches it away, placing it on her lap.

'Look at the kind of lifestyle I have. You couldn't get enough of this place last night,' Karen says, observing her apartment with a smile on her face. A fake smile.

'And now I've changed my mind,' Jason says.

'Yeah?'

'All of this stuff, it means nothing without someone special to share it with,' he says, speaking from bitter experience. He had a beautiful house a few years back, but once his wife and children left, it wasn't so beautiful anymore. It was cold, dull, stale. Just like the pokey flat he's got above his bar.

'Things are fine the way they are. I've got everything I could ever need,' she says.

'Yeah, a flash car, a posh apartment, and all the designer clothes a woman could dream of,' Jason says, watching her until her eyes meet his. 'And a heart that's broken.'

'It's fully functioning, thank you.' Karen shakes her head. She might have changed in many ways but she's still as stubborn as ever.

'Wouldn't you rather be poor and happy than rich and alone? Don't you remember how we used to be? We didn't need anything but each other, just sitting in the park having a picnic or going for walk. We didn't need a plasma screen or a convertible. I needed you and you needed me, that was it,' Jason reminds her, and he can tell she still shares his happy memories as a smile appears on her pale face.

'Such a shame you threw it all away,' she says, her smile suddenly disappearing, as if embarrassed for feeling the way she did.

CHAPTER TWENTY
1997

Now that they were alone, Jason watched as Karen slid down the wall until she was crouched on the floor, her knees pulled up to her chest.

'I know it must be hard to believe but it's not how it looks. It meant nothing. I don't love her. In fact, I don't even know how it happened. We were having a bit of harmless banter one minute and the next we were in bed. It just happened, Karen,' Jason told her, pained by the expression on her face: she looked hurt, exhausted, almost tortured.

'You've completely forgotten, haven't you?' Karen said, not looking at him.

'Didn't you hear what I just said?' Jason asked, stunned that she had not yet raised her voice.

'What day is it today?' Karen asked.

'Tuesday,' Jason said, letting out an involuntary laugh, unable to understand where these questions were coming from.

'Now really isn't the time to be doing a little comedy routine. I waited for you. They even delayed my appointment by ten minutes to see if you'd turn up,' Karen said, the penny finally dropping for Jason.

'The scan. Oh god, I'm such an idiot,' Jason said, inhaling loudly, feeling his heart plummeting as if falling through his whole body, down to the tips of his toes.

'Understatement of the decade,' Karen said, rather harshly, and Jason couldn't blame her, given the circumstances. He felt ashamed.

'How was it? We'll have to book another one and I promise I'll be there. I can't wait to see it on the screen again. I bet it looks so big compared to last time,' Jason said, suddenly feeling a surge of adrenaline through his body, excited for the future, just the three of them. 'Did they tell you if it's a boy or girl? They can tell at twenty-one weeks, can't they?'

'If you'd bothered to show your face, you'd have heard the nurse say there was no heartbeat,' Karen said.

'What?'

'I lost it at twenty weeks. I have to go back tomorrow to deliver her. They wanted me to stay in but I discharged myself,' Karen explained, and Jason could see her desperately trying to hold back the tears.

'It's a girl?' Jason asked, shocked, feeling as though everything else in the world was moving in slow motion around them, yet he was unable to take anything in.

'Was,' Karen corrected him, her voice quivering.

'I'll be there with you tomorrow,' Jason told her, keen to make up for his terrible mistake. He had to make it up to her. He had to fight for her.

'I'd rather go alone,' Karen said.

'I don't think that's a good idea, sweetheart,' he said softly.

'And I don't think you're in any position to lecture me, do you?' Karen said, almost spitting her words at him.

'She was my baby too,' Jason said, tears filling his eyes.

Karen looked at Jason for a moment, the two of them connecting in their devastation before she pulled herself up from the ground. Jason watched her place a delicate hand on her small but perfectly formed baby bump and his heart broke for her, knowing she'd had to go through something so traumatic all on her own. He wanted to hold her, to comfort her, but he *knew she'd push him away, so he stayed rooted to the spot as Karen walked down the corridor, as far from him as she could possibly get.*

CHAPTER TWENTY-ONE
Present Day

Coming through from the kitchen, Jason finds Karen in the corner of the room near the answer machine. The red light has been flashing since they got back from the party last night but it seems Karen can't, and won't, avoid it anymore.

"Where are you? Why aren't you picking up? I know you're home. You wouldn't have gone out alone. How sad would that look? A woman of your age turning up to a party all on your own. Come on Karen, pick up the phone . . ." Jason hears Paul's voice come out of the answer machine. Cold, cruel, intimidating. If he isn't a bully then he really doesn't know what is.

Karen has her back to Jason, her arms folded across her chest with her head bowed slightly. If he ever came face to face with Paul, there was so much he wanted to say to him. He'd got himself the most perfect wife, so kind and so beautiful, yet he chose to mistreat her, staying away for weeks on end, leaving her to fend for herself. Jason knows she's more than capable, but it's still not right. Paul should have gone to the party with her. He should be here, by her side.

He knows he would've been, if he had been lucky enough to become her husband.

Karen's body shakes and Jason can hear the faint sound of muffled sobs as he walks over to her, needing to comfort her. He reaches past her and turns the answer machine off, hoping this will offer her a little respite from the torment.

'You okay?' Jason asks, putting a supportive hand on her back. 'I know I've said it already, but I'll keep saying it until you listen. Leave him, Karen.'

'And be with you?' Karen says, quickly wiping the tears from her eyes as if that will cover up how upset she is.

'I'm not saying leave him and come to me – although believe me, that's all I've ever wanted. I'm just saying don't stay with a man who hurts you and talks to you like something he found on the bottom of his shoe,' Jason says. 'Don't settle for anything less than the best, Karen. I'm begging you.'

'It's not that easy. Amelia would want us to be together,' Karen says, sighing.

'Amelia?' Jason says.

Hearing it again has a weird effect on Jason. It's haunting. The name they had picked out for their child. The child they never got to meet. Amelia for a girl. Archie for a boy.

'Our daughter. Mine and Paul's, I mean. She's at boarding school at the moment,' she tells Jason.

'I didn't realise you were a mother,' Jason says. There's not a single trace of her daughter in the entire apartment; even her bedroom is the "spare room" with the walls painted a dull magnolia with plain bedding. No princesses or fairy lights. No boy band posters plastered on the walls.

Karen opens the top drawer of the side table beside the sofa. It's full of photos and Jason wonders if there's any from when they were kids. She takes one from the collection and shows it to him. It's a lovely photograph of a young girl, perhaps about eleven years old, with a smile just like Karen's and big, bright eyes – again, just like her mother.

'She's beautiful, just like you,' Jason says.

'My pride and joy,' Karen says, a beaming smile on her face. He can tell she's very proud of her child.

'So why do you have her photo hidden away?' Jason asks.

'Paul's into all this minimalist stuff. Photos and ornaments are just clutter to him,' Karen tells him, immediately putting the photo back and closing the drawer as if she is scared of him returning at any moment.

'You shouldn't stay with Paul for Amelia's sake. She'd want to come home and see her mother with a smile on her face.'

'Times like this, I'd give anything to go back in time.'

CHAPTER TWENTY-TWO
Present Day

Danielle is following Bradley around the house. It's not the first time she's done this; in fact, it's pretty much a regular occurrence now. Everywhere he goes, she goes, giving him a big long list of reasons why he can't go into work or for a pint with friends. Today is no different.

Actually, today is different. Bradley isn't going to work. Although the less Danielle knows about his plans, the better. She'd call him insensitive, leaving her on a day like today, but he's not. He's a good husband, and under any other circumstances he'd be by her side all day. But today is different. Today he needs to put himself first.

Bradley goes into the bedroom to put on the clean shirt he'd set out on the bed earlier that morning, and he tries not to smile. He'd been looking forward to the school reunion for months and to then miss it was a big disappointment. Today he would finally get to see them all again, remember the good times and, maybe, if they were lucky, get their friendship back.

Within seconds, Danielle comes into the room, watching as he changes shirts.

'I can't believe you're going into work,' Danielle says, rolling her eyes.

'It can't be helped. I'm on call,' Bradley tells her, but he knows she's feeling anything but understanding. She never is, this time of year.

'Today of all days,' she sighs as she bows her head, trying to pull at his heartstrings. It's the oldest trick in the book and, to be honest, he's growing a little tired of it.

'I won't be long.'

'Meaning you'll be gone all day,' she says, her voice laced with frustration.

Bradley pauses for a moment, keeping his eyes locked with hers, hoping she'll back down, but as he reaches for his pager on the bedside table, she gets there first, gripping it in her hand.

'Come on, don't be like this,' Bradley says, taking it from her hand. She's holding on so tight he has to peel her fingers away, one by one, her fists clenched so tightly.

'You know how hard it is for me and my mum. You should be here supporting us,' Danielle says as she goes through the pockets of Bradley's jacket.

'I came with you to the graveyard,' Bradley reminds her. He does feel guilty.

'And that's it, is it? Husband duties over for the day?' she asks, shooting him a nasty glare.

'You knew about my career when we first met. I'm a doctor. I can't pick and choose when I go in as much as other people can. The public rely on me,' he tells her, taking something else from her hand: his car keys.

'Your wife relies on you,' she says. She says this most days, not just today. Bradley hates it when she says things like this to him. He does his best to be here when she needs him, but how can he do that when he's working? He needs to work to keep the roof over their heads, to put food on the table, and to pay for their appointments.

'I'll be a couple of hours. Hopefully. But I'll definitely be home for dinner,' Bradley calls over his shoulder as he rushes downstairs and out of the house. He has to admit, he does feel bad for lying to her, but it really is for her own good. She just wouldn't see it that way.

*****

After finishing the mug of strong coffee that Jason has made for her, to help get rid of her headache, she's persuaded to join him in visiting Jessica. He's told her that Jessica gave him her address and phone number last night. He'd made a note of them both in his mobile and as he lifted the screen to show Karen, she had been overcome with another huge wave of jealousy.

It got her thinking: if Jason hadn't lost his keys last night, would he have gone into his bar, into his flat, never seeing her again? Would he have just kept in contact with Jessica? The very thought that she'd never see Jason again brought a tear to her eye, so she cast her fears aside and just offered him a smile.

Although she has yet to be convinced that their visit to Jessica's place is a good thing, here she is, driving her convertible Jaguar, the breeze lacing her hair as she heads towards Jessica's home with Jason in the passenger seat.

'I'm still not sure about this,' Karen says as her hands tighten around the steering wheel. Who would have thought she'd be so nervous, visiting a woman who was once her best friend? It's a strange feeling.

'It'll take your mind off your so-called husband,' Jason says, seething.

'You really don't like him, do you?' Karen says. She has to admit though, she quite likes the fact he's so resentful of her husband. She likes that Jason's jealous.

'I hate him for the way he treats you. Don't you?' he asks her.

'No. I think that's the worst part about it,' Karen says, letting out a sigh as she catches sight of her wedding ring.

'Well, this will cheer you up. A few hours with Jess,' he says.

'Somehow, I don't think it will.' Karen shakes her head before looking at the cars on the other side of the road. A constant stream of traffic. No chance to do a U-turn.

'She's our friend. Or at least she was before . . .' His voice trails off and Karen knows he's feeling guilty for the way things ended at university. 'I know things haven't been easy between you and Jess, but maybe this can be a fresh start for everyone.'

'Aren't you nervous though?' Karen asks, gulping hard to stop the tremble in her voice.

'Course I am, but last night was amazing. It might not have gone to plan, but just seeing you again means a lot to me,' Jason says.

'Big softy really, aren't you, Jay?' Karen teases him, unable to hide her smile.

'I mean it. I felt something last night. I felt like we were getting our friendship back,' Jason smiles back; the sweetest, most handsome smile Karen's ever known. Some things really haven't changed.

'You must have been at a different party.'

'I know you liked it too. You just won't admit it,' Jason says. 'I want to track Bradley down too. Him not being there was the one thing that stopped last night being perfect . . .'

'And Veronica doing a runner,' Karen says. Karen hasn't stopped thinking about her since the party. Her blood-shot eyes, the dirt under her nails, the staining on her teeth, the weird noises she made when she breathed in and out.

'We'll find her.'

'In a city as big as London, you really think we'll just spot her wandering the streets?'

'It might not be easy but we'll do it. I really want us to get back to how we were,' he says, placing his hand on Karen's leg, just for a moment, before he removes it again.

'Me too,' Karen says, nodding her head gently so her hair falls forward, hiding her cheeks, which she suspects have flushed a light shade of pink. 'I'm sorry about last night.'

'It's fine. I'm just enjoying being with you again,' Jason says.

For a few moments, they reside peacefully in one another's company, listening to the muffled sound of the radio. The song ends and another begins almost immediately after. A song that means something to both of them. A song that takes them right back.

When they were teenagers, it was their soundtrack. Any occasion, any time they could blast some music out, they'd play "Living on A Prayer" by Bon Jovi. It was a favourite with all five of them, and they knew every single word, and would sing, or rather scream them at the top of their lungs.

Jason reaches across and turns up the volume. Karen watches him as he smiles. That big, cheeky grin she loves so much. Then she catches a quick glimpse of herself in his mirrored aviators and she can see she's smiling too. A real smile. The first proper smile for as long as she can remember. Not forced or fake. Just natural.

'It's like we're eighteen again,' Jason laughs, obviously remembering one of their many road trips – although they were hardly road trips. It was more driving round the local estates, with the volume as high as it would go, not caring if they annoyed the neighbours. As long as they were all together, they were invincible.

CHAPTER TWENTY-THREE
Present Day

Denise, in her early sixties, with cropped silver hair and a face that looked older than her years, sits at her kitchen table. There's a steaming mug of tea in front of her and the radio is on quietly in the background, but the only thing she can focus on this morning is the newspaper in front of her.

20 YEARS ON AND STILL NO JUSTICE

The headline was spot on. How could something so tragic have happened all those years ago and not one single person be arrested in connection? It was murder, no doubt about it. He wouldn't have sustained those head injuries from an accidental fall. It was done on purpose. But who would have had a grievance against him? He was a kind, patient and well-loved member of staff, and one of the more popular lecturers amongst the students.

People say that time heals but, for her, it hadn't. It had only deepened her grief. With no arrests, the investigation closed, and people going about their daily lives, she felt as though she had failed her husband. She hadn't got justice. He hadn't had justice.

It didn't make any sense.

It wasn't fair.

Isn't fair.

CHAPTER TWENTY-FOUR
2007

Danielle and Denise were in the bridal suite of a hotel, each with a glass of champagne. They'd planned for it to be a relaxed night, just the two of them, before Danielle's wedding to Bradley the following day, but Denise hadn't been able to keep the sad news she'd received just twelve hours earlier from her daughter. It would have been cruel to let her go off on her honeymoon for two weeks, oblivious to the fact that the police were no longer hunting for her father's killer.

'They're closing the case?' Danielle asked, her eyes filling with tears, both of anger and of sadness.

'I know it's difficult. We all want answers. Us, his friends, his colleagues . . .' Denise said.

'I don't care about his friends and colleagues. I care about us. We deserve closure,' Danielle replied.

'It's been ten years, Danielle. The police have tried their hardest,' Denise said, taking her daughter's shaking hand.

'So you're willing to give up?' Danielle asked.

'People can't run forever. One day they will be found. I really believe that. You must too.'

Denise waited for Danielle to speak; instead, she finished every last drop of champagne in her glass and was about to pour herself another when Denise placed a delicate hand on her arm, stopping her.

'It's a big day tomorrow, sweetheart. The biggest of your life. You should get some rest,' Denise said softly.

'I'm dreading walking down the aisle,' Danielle admitted,

putting the champagne bottle down and looking straight into her mother's eyes.

'You're not having second thoughts, are you?' Denise asked.

'No, of course not. It'll just feel lonely without Dad giving me away,' Danielle said.

'You'll never be lonely, Danielle. I'll always be by your side,' Denise reassured her, letting Danielle cuddle up to her as if she was a small child again.

CHAPTER TWENTY-FIVE
Present Day

A knock at the door interrupts Jessica's housework. She's a little annoyed. The place is a mess, thanks to Natalie's party last night, and she needs to have it looking presentable ready for her visitor later this afternoon. Taking her hands from the warm, soapy water, leaving the dirty dishes to soak, she rushes to answer to door, drying her hands as she does so. It's probably sales people or one of the neighbours coming to complain about something.

Jessica opens the door to find Jason and Karen in front of her. She's shocked. Despite swapping details with Jason at the party last night, she never expected him to call or visit. Not now he has Karen back in his life. She's all he ever wanted. Not her.

'Hi,' Jessica says, finally breaking the silence.

'Hi, how are you?' Jason asks, offering a friendly smile.

'I didn't expect to see you again,' Jessica says, although she keeps her gaze firmly on Karen, who is cowering behind Jason.

'Have w-we come at a bad time? We can go. W-we should go,' Karen stutters, looking as if she's ready to do a runner.

'No, it's fine. It's a surprise, that's all. Come in,' Jessica says, holding the door open a little wider.

Jason glances at Karen, perhaps indicating for her to go in first, but she remains rooted to the spot. It's obvious she's not here by choice as Jason takes the lead, coming into the living room with Karen walking behind him, like his shadow.

Jessica closes the door and edges a little closer to them. Not too close though as Karen glare at her, as if warning her to keep her distance from Jason.

'So, how are you feeling this morning?' Jason asks.

'A bit rough, I won't lie,' Jessica admits, referring to her alcohol-induced headache. 'It's great to see you both. I was going to try and contact you actually. I had a call from Bradley.'

'You did? How is he?' Karen asks, her eyes suddenly lighting up. They were always very close at university. They all were.

'Okay, I think. He said he was sorry for missing the party and that he's on his way over here,' Jessica tells them.

'How did he know how to find you?' Karen asks, looking right at Jessica for the first time since the reunion.

'He said something about one of his mates being in the police force. He owed Bradley a favour so he got him to track me down,' Jessica lies; truth is, he didn't give a reason, just called out of the blue. She wasn't going to ask questions. His call meant they're one step closer to reuniting properly.

'It'll be good to see him,' Jason says, grinning. He'll be glad of a bit of male influence instead of being surrounded by women, like he was last night.

'I don't suppose you've heard from Veronica?' Karen asks.

'I don't think she has an entry in yellow pages, what with being on the streets and everything,' Jessica says with a smile, trying to make light of the situation. Karen doesn't return the smile. 'Anyway, can I get anyone a coffee?'

'Yeah, that'd be great. One sugar, cheers,' Jason says.

'Karen?' Jessica asks.

'Black, no sugar. Thanks,' Karen says, a little bluntly, and Jessica walks out of the room and into the kitchen.

*****

After a few moments, Karen follows her, although she wonders how you can even call this tiny space a kitchen. It's the size of her walk-in wardrobe and at least three times smaller than her own. Jessica's stood by the kettle, making the drinks. Karen know she's aware of her presence as her eyes flick to her and then back to the hot beverages on the work surface.

'You okay?' Jess asks, without looking at Karen.

'Fine. You?'

'Not great, but nothing an early night won't sort out,' she says, sighing as she turns to face Karen. She looks exhausted. 'Look, I know I'm not exactly your favourite person, but for now can we just try and get on? Bradley's on his way and I'm sure he wouldn't want to see us arguing.'

'You're right. Spending time with Jason has made me realise how much I've missed you all. We need to put our problems behind us and move on. Or at least try,' Karen says, although her feelings are still uncertain. One minute she wants to be back with them; the next she wants to run away.

'Do you mean that?' Jess asks, a smile emerging on her lips.

'We're not kids anymore. This is real life, not the playground,' Karen says.

'Friends?' Jess holds out her hand. The nails are short, but not bitten. No nail varnish. Not like Karen's, which are long, perfectly manicured, and painted a deep shade of red.

'Friends.'

Before she even has time to realise what she's doing, Karen pulls Jessica into a hug. She can tell by her tense body that Jessica is a little taken back by her gesture and so is she, if she's honest.

'Have I walked back into the wrong flat?' Jason asks, coming into the room, prompting Karen to pull away from Jessica.

'He's phoned work to say he won't be in. Still a skiver,' Karen says to Jessica, smiling, knowing it will wind Jason up. She used to do it all time when . . .well, when things were easier.

'Oi! I'll have you know I work very hard,' he says, laughing, nudging Karen a little.

'Yeah?'

'Yeah, it's tiring running your own business.'

'Isn't it just. You don't have to tell me, Jase, I own a salon.'

There's silence for a while. Karen's not sure exactly how long as she can't seem to remove her eyes from Jason. He eventually breaks eye contact and she wonders why, until she sees him offering Jessica a kind smile. Yet again she's come between them.

'What is it you do, Jess?' Jason asks.

'I'm a cleaner. I work at a hotel in town. It's rubbish compared to what you two do, but you can't be fussy these days, can you?' she says quickly, as if she is ashamed. Jess has always been the same, thinking no-one will be interested, thinking she's worth less than everyone else.

'It takes all kinds of people to make up this world. You've got a teenager to support, that's the main thing,' Jason reassures her and Karen watches them exchange kind smiles, clenching her fists.

'I wish I'd done more with my life,' Jessica says, shaking her head, clearly full of regret.

'Don't put yourself down. You've got a decent life and being a parent is one of the best things you could have done with it,' Jason replies. 'I bet you're a fantastic mother.'

'Always were a charmer, weren't you?' Jessica smiles shyly, bowing her head shyly.

Just when Jessica thinks things are going well, Karen storms out of the kitchen so fast her feet barely touch the ground, and within a matter of seconds they hear the front door slam.

'Did I do something wrong?' Jess asks, worried.

'No, don't worry. She's having a tough time right now. I think she's finding it all a bit overwhelming,' Jason explains, wanting to calm her nerves. He can tell she's still torturing herself over what they did. She's scared of Karen, anyone can see that.

*****

Coming out of the petrol station shop, juggling a bottle of water, his wallet and his car keys in his hands, Bradley feels his phone vibrate in his pocket before it starts ringing loudly, irritating his ears. He knows who it'll be so he doesn't bother to check the screen as he rests his belongings on top of his car, pulling it from his pocket.

Bradley barely has the phone to his ear before she starts at him: 'Where are you?'

'I'm fine thanks, babe, how are you?' Bradley says, perhaps a bit too sarcastically.

'Don't be like that with me! I just rang the hospital and they said you weren't even down to work today. You lied to me!' she says.

He knows he'll be in for it when he gets home. And Danielle's mother will have a field day nagging him about his responsibilities as a husband.

'Yeah, I swapped with someone the other day. It slipped my mind until I went in this morning. I won't . . . erm . . . I will be back late tonight though,' Bradley lies, tripping over his words as he does so.

'Why? Where are you?' Danielle asks.

'There's something I need to do. Why did you ring the hospital anyway? Are you okay?' Bradley asks, suddenly worried, although it wouldn't surprise him if she was just checking up on him.

'Oh yeah, greatest day of my life.'

'Stop it, Danielle. I know today is hard for you but you've got to stop taking it out on me.'

'Sorry,' she says, taking a deep breath. 'I managed to get us an appointment tomorrow lunchtime.'

'Right . . .' Bradley says, his heart sinking a little. He thought they had an agreement.

'It is still what you want isn't it?' she asks.

'Of course. I've got to go. I'll see you later,' Bradley says, keen to finish the call as soon as possible.

'I love you,' Danielle says sweetly.

'Yeah, you too,' Bradley replies before ending the call and climbing into his car. He's got somewhere important to be.

CHAPTER TWENTY-SIX
Present Day

Leaning against the wall, the harsh feel of the brick clashes with the smooth material of Karen's designer blouse. She'll have to get it dry-cleaned straight away. Paul will go mad if he comes home to find her clothes in a state. Though God knows why. He's rarely here to see her wear them anyway.

She takes one last drag of her cigarette, the nicotine a great source of comfort in her time of need, before throwing it to the ground and stamping on it. Her heel squeaks a little as it rubs against the pavement, sending a shiver down her spine. She takes another cigarette from the packet and lights it, immediately taking a long drag.

Karen is brought from her thoughts by a person walking by. Looking up, she sees it's a young girl, perhaps in her mid-teens. Pretty and petite with big brown eyes. But she gives off a vibe of being strong and confident beyond her years.

'Bad day?' the girl asks, stopping in her tracks.

'Is it any of your business?' Karen snaps.

'Just trying to be friendly.'

'Sorry.'

'Are you a friend of Jessica's?' the girl asks.

'Yeah. Or at least I used to be,' Karen says, taking a drag of her cigarette to ease her nerves.

'So, are you Karen or Veronica?' she asks.

'Karen Gallagher.'

'Nice to finally meet you Karen Gallagher. I'm Natalie Palmer. Mum's told me loads about you,' Natalie says, smiling at her. A cheeky grin, full of mischief.

'Mum?' Karen says, although she had already worked it out. It's strange. She feels as if she's seen Natalie before, although there are no photographs up in Jessica's flat.

'Has she not mentioned me?' Natalie asks.

'We've not been here long. We've got a lot of catching up to do . . .' Karen says, her voice trailing off, dreading the thought of having to go back into the flat.

Natalie bows her head, obviously not sure of what to say as she shuffles from one foot to another. Like someone else Karen knows. She takes another drag of her cigarette, needing to distract herself.

'Is Jason with you?' Natalie asks, breaking the silence.

'Yeah. How? . . .' Karen asks, frowning in confusion. For a girl she's never met, she knows a lot about her life.

'Mum told me about you two; said you split up at uni. She didn't say you'd got back together though,' Natalie says.

'That's because we're not,' Karen tells her.

'Oh, sorry,' she says, seeming a little awkward.

'It's fine. I've had twenty years to get used to it,' Karen says, letting out a little sigh. You'd think that spending twenty years apart from someone would make your feelings disappear, but in her case, it had only made them stronger. Not that she'd admit it.

Karen looks Natalie up and down, taking in her outfit. For a young girl, she's got brilliant fashion sense. Teenagers are often a bit mismatched, struggling to find a style that suits them, but she's got it spot on, stood there in her skinny jeans, ankle boots and off the shoulder top. Simple but stylish.

She's got long brown hair, which falls around her shoulders. It's not in any particular style, just loose and a little ruffled. Perhaps she'd done it to try and create volume. She's also wearing no make-up. Not that Karen can see anyway. She doesn't need it. She's a natural beauty with clear skin and a sparkle in her eyes. Karen reckons she'd left the flat at the crack of dawn, leaving little time for a beauty regime. Or maybe she was out all night. Karen was at her age.

'What?' she asks, self-consciously, running her fingers through her hair as if she thinks Karen's mentally criticising her.

'You're a very pretty young girl,' Karen says, keeping her gaze firmly fixed on her face, the eyes she recognises and that mischievous grin.

'Thanks.' She smiles softly, looking just like Jessica did when she used to receive compliments all those years ago. Touched and flattered, if not a little shocked by the kind words.

Neither of them speak for a while, but when Karen takes a couple of drags of her cigarette, she notices Natalie eyeing up the packet in her hand. They've only just met, yet Karen can read her like a book. Something else that's familiar.

'Not a chance, darlin'. Cheeky little thing, aren't you? Nothing like your mother was at your age,' Karen says as an involuntary giggle escapes her lips.

'Really?'

'She was so shy. So scared of life. She would never have tried to nick a fag off someone. She tried to break away from it a couple of times, but she couldn't. It's who she is.'

'Veronica was the rebellious one, I take it?'

'What makes you think that?'

'You seem too cool and calm, like you have everything under control.'

'Don't be fooled by the fact I've got a bit of money in my pocket. Life hasn't been easy for me. I went off the rails when I was a bit younger than you,' Karen explains. People often get the wrong impression of her. They see where she lives, her business, her car and her designer clothes, and they assume she's got a life of luxury. Most people dream of having a life like hers, fantasising about winning the lottery so they can fund it all. But Karen's not most people, and this isn't luxury to her.

'What happened?' Natalie asks, seeming genuinely interested in what Karen has to say.

It's nice to talk to someone of her age. It makes Karen think of Amelia, although she's a few years younger than Natalie is. She wishes she was home with her, having normal mother-daughter conversations. She can't remember the last time they talked . . . properly talked.

'I was saved,' Karen says, taking one last drag of her cigarette, feeling the burn of the toxins travel all the way down her throat, before letting it fall to the ground, stamping it out like she had with the last.

CHAPTER TWENTY-SEVEN
Present Day

Driving through the city streets, the sound of his ringing mobile phone clashing with the radio, Bradley is brought from his thoughts. His phone is lying on the passenger seat, where Danielle usually sits, and the shrill ringing coming from the speakers makes it sounds as though his wife is actually present in the car. If she's not here to moan at him in person, she makes sure she does it by phone-call instead. As he stops at a set of traffic lights, he throws his phone into the glove compartment and turns off the radio, bringing blissful silence to his car.

It's not her fault, though, the way things are. Anyone going through the same situation would feel the way she does: angry; confused, empty. She's tried so hard, over the years, to fill the gap left in her heart, but nothing ever really comes close. Bradley tries to help her in any way he can, but there isn't much that can bring her comfort, especially at this time of year. Although he understands why she feels the way she does, he finds it hard to put himself in her shoes. Having grown up in a loving, stable family with happily married parents and two brothers, he's never had to experience the things she has.

It wasn't always like this. When Bradley first met Danielle, she was so at happy, so at ease. She'd always had her demons, but she could deal with them better back then, and when they first got together, she was rarely seen without a smile. Now, it's rare to see her smile. To hear her laugh. He misses her laugh. This morning she'd dissolved into tears pretty much every hour from the moment she woke up.

The sound of a car horn startles Bradley, immediately bringing him from his daze, and as he glances in the rear-view mirror, he's confronted with the line of traffic that's built behind him. If the rest of the drivers have got faces like the one directly behind him, he's in serious trouble. Anger etched on his face, the man driving the posh Audi is waving his arms around and shouting, despite the fact Bradley can't hear him. He must have been day-dreaming longer than he thought. Happens a lot. It's the only peace he seems to get.

Releasing the handbrake, he sets off once again in search of Jessica's flat. The butterflies in his stomach are fluttering so fast he feels like he might have to pull over on the side of the road. It's a strange feeling. When he was a kid, he'd think nothing of going to one of their houses; in fact, it felt like each one of them had five homes. But not anymore. It feels like he's meeting with a stranger, and it makes him wish he'd been at last night's reunion even more.

He'd spent all night by Danielle's side, trying to imagine what his friends would be like now. He wondered if Jessica ever managed to find her Mr Right. She was longing for a boyfriend back then. She'd see Karen and Jason together, and Veronica with her string of male admirers, and she'd wish the same could happen to her. Maybe that's why she did what she did, why she betrayed Karen so badly.

He imagines Veronica's still got a load of admirers, all vying for her attention, but he hopes she's found someone to settle down with. She was fun and beautiful when she was younger, loved showing off and flirting. But it was clear to them all that the reason for having a different date every week was because she was searching for The One. Not that she'd ever admit it.

Karen was always the most glamorous, most ambitious of the five of them. She's probably some high-flying businesswoman with millions in the bank and a loving family who completely worship her. It wouldn't surprise Bradley. Not one bit.

He wonders if Jason has moved on from Karen, found someone else to love. Maybe he's become a father. Or he could have searched until he found Karen and they could have been living happily ever after for the last twenty years. Bradley's not so sure "happy ever after exists" beyond the fairy tales, but if it does, he hopes its happened for his friends. All of them.

CHAPTER TWENTY-EIGHT
Present Day

Karen goes into the flat, following Natalie, who keeps her head down, muttering something under her breath when she sees Jessica, before shutting herself in her bedroom. Jessica doesn't seem overly bothered, engrossed in a conversation with Jason. They're sat close to one another, giggling away like a couple of kids.

'Sounds like you're having a laugh,' Karen says, raising her eyebrows at them in suspicion. She hates seeing them together.

Karen never thought anything of it when they were growing up together. She was never jealous of the two of them. They used to do everything together, and if two of them were left alone, it was entirely innocent. Not anymore. Now they've got history, *real* history, and it hurts.

'I think I've still got some washing up to do,' Jessica mutters before making a quick dash for the kitchen, closing the door firmly behind her. Typical.

'I know she's the one you want,' Karen says, turning back to Jason.

'You don't know anything,' Jason says.

'That makes me feel great. Thanks,' Karen replies, her words embedded with sarcasm.

'No, if you knew anything you'd know you're the one. You're the only woman I've ever truly loved,' he tells her.

'Is that your guilty conscience talking?'

'It's the truth. I know you feel the same way.'

'I'm a married woman.'

'He doesn't love you.'

'No man has ever loved me. I've got used to it by now,' Karen shrugs. Considering she's only ever been with two men her whole life, she's had her heart broken a lot.

'I love you. I always will,' he says, trying to take Karen's hand, but she rejects his gesture, folding her arms across her chest.

'It didn't always feel that way,' she says, casting her mind back to that fateful day at university. Losing her baby. Their baby. Walking into the flat. Walking into the bedroom. Seeing him. Seeing Jessica. She blinks hard, not wanting to cry in front of Jason.

'I made mistakes, but I was young and that's all they were. Mistakes,' he says.

'Those mistakes broke my heart,' Karen says, although she doesn't think she can make him feel any more guilty than he already does.

'You have to believe me when I say I love you. Come on, Karen, I don't know what else to say. We were getting on so well this morning,' he says, the tone of his voice changing to that of pure desperation.

'Until you insisted we come and visit Jess. I saw the way you were looking at her. Now I know why you were so keen to see her again.'

'What do you want me to do? Give her evils all day? I think she had enough of that from you last night.'

'Why would you want me?'

'Why wouldn't I?'

'You've got a readymade family here with Jess.'

'What?' Jason asks, looking completely baffled.

'Natalie's a gorgeous-looking girl, isn't she?' Karen says, keeping her eyes locked with his, wanting to see his reaction.

'Takes after Jess. And before you start having a go, that wasn't me confessing my "love" for her,' Jason says.

'She's got your smile,' Karen tells him. Even the thought of a child baring a resemblance to Jason makes her stomach churn. A child that's not hers.

'Don't be stupid,' he says, shaking his head.

'She's got your cheeky personality too. And your eyes,' Karen says, refusing to back down. She knows she's right.

'She hasn't,' he says, although Karen can see guilt written all over his face.

'I'd know those eyes anywhere, Jason,' Karen replies.

'That doesn't prove anything. Lots of p-people have brown eyes. Doesn't m-mean they're linked in any way,' Jason says, his words spilling from his mouth so fast that he stutters occasionally. His eyes are fixed firmly on Karen but his mind is elsewhere, whirring with panic and angst.

'Then why do you look so worried?' Karen asks, her heart sinking. Despite making the connection herself, she'd hoped that Jason would put her mind at rest; instead, he's confirmed her fears.

'I'm not,' he says, although he's broken eye contact with her. A classic sign of a liar.

'Look me in the eye and tell me that last night was the first time you'd seen Jess since uni.'

Karen watches him. His face. His mouth is open slightly. His breath heavy. Short and sharp as if he is panicking. He licks his lips, another classic sign of lying, but still Karen clings to the hope that he's stuck for what to say and not that she was right with her suspicions.

She doesn't want to cry. She doesn't want to break down. She hates showing weakness, but when she moves her gaze to his eyes, he immediately breaks eye contact again, looking at the scruffy carpet instead of at Karen.

'I hope you'll be very happy together,' Karen says, her body trembling, doing her best to keep her emotions under control.

Jason tries to take her hand but she snatches it away. She can physically feel the anger bubbling away inside herself. She despises him for making her feel like this again.

Karen leaves the flat, keeping her head down, focusing on the concrete steps that clash with her shoes as she makes her way back down to the car park. In the distance, she can just about hear Jason's voice, although she can't make out whether he's pleading with her or sharing another joke with Jessica. Maybe they're all talking, the three of them: Jason, Jessica and their daughter.

'Well, well, well . . .' a voice calls out, making Karen look up from the ground as she reaches her car.

'Bradley?' Karen gasps, seeing him for the first time in twenty years. He's still as good-looking as ever, leaning against his car. 'Wow, look at you! You look great, all done up in your fancy shirt. Nice to see one of us has done well in life.'

'Doesn't look like you've done too badly yourself,' he says, glancing at her Jaguar gleaming in the lunchtime sun.

'Don't let the flash car fool you,' Karen says.

'You look amazing. Come here,' he replies, pulling her into a hug. He always did this when she was feeling down. Perhaps he's sensed that she's upset. 'How was the reunion?'

'One of the hardest nights of my life,' Karen says, breaking from the hug.

'Are things still difficult between you and Jess?' he asks.

'You could say that,' Karen nods weakly.

'And that's why you're doing a runner, yeah?'

'I'm leaving, not doing a "runner". There's a difference,' Karen says, although he's spot on with his observation. She wishes she could run away. From Jessica. From Paul. But not from Jason.

'The last time you left it was because of Jason and Jess. You shouldn't let them have that much control over you,' Bradley says. He always tried to help her out when they were younger, protecting her from being hurt. In fact, he tried to protect them all. It seems some things haven't changed.

CHAPTER TWENTY-NINE
1997

It was a Monday, around lunchtime, and despite several people rushing from one building to another, Karen remained focused on the gates. Once she'd stepped through them, she'd never have to return. She'd be free.

Reaching her destination, passing through the gates, the murmur of excitable voices and laughter diminished with each step, and Karen breathed a sigh of relief. That relief was short-lived, however, when she found Jason hanging around on the corner of a nearby housing estate. They used to meet here all the time when they were together.

She used to run as fast as she could from her lecture so she could see her boyfriend as early as possible. But seeing him here now broke her heart and instead of running to him, she wanted to run from him.

'You'll get a bad reputation, standing on a street corner like that,' Karen said, not bothering to look at him as she passed, her arms folded tightly across her chest.

'We need to talk,' he said.

'No, we don't.' Karen shook her head, trying to pick up her pace. A hard feat as she was still feeling tired and run-down following her ordeal a few days previously.

'I've been trying to call you for three days. Where have you been?' he asked, pulling her round so they were facing each other – although she still refused eye contact.

'My mum's. Not that it's any of your business,' Karen told him.

'I went to your mum's. She said she hadn't seen you either,' he said.

'That's because I told her to say that. I didn't want to see you,' Karen replied, and despite the fact she wasn't looking at him, she knew he'd be heartbroken by her statement. But at least he'd know how she felt.

'How did it go at the hospital?' he asked.

'Great, I loved it. Had the time of my life,' Karen snapped, her words loaded with sarcasm.

'Grow up, Karen! I know you're angry with me, and you have every right to be, but she would have been my daughter too. You should have let me be there for you,' Jason said.

'I didn't want you there. I don't want you or my friendship with Jess. It's finished. All of it. It's all gone,' Karen said, although that couldn't have been further from the truth. She did want him there. When she was at her most scared, it was his name that she called. It was him that she wanted by her side, holding her hand, but she knew she couldn't give in to him so easily. She refused to be treated like a doormat. She deserved more. If only she knew the direction her life would go in.

'We need to sit down and talk things through. We see each other every day,' he said.

'We don't have to,' Karen told him.

'You can run and hide at your mum's house for a couple of weeks if that's what you want, but one day you'll bump into me or Jess and wish we'd sorted things out,' Jason replied.

'If I have my way I'll never see either of you again,' Karen said before finally locking eyes with him. 'I'm leaving.'

'Don't be stupid, Karen, you don't have to do that,' he said as he tried to take her hands, which had fallen to her side a few moments earlier, only for her to reject his gesture.

'I'm sick of you telling me what to do. I'm twenty-one years old and I'm capable of making my own decisions. I'm leaving and I'm never coming back. This place holds too many bad memories,' Karen said, securing her arms across her chest again as a shiver trickled down her spine.

'So just think of the good memories instead,' he said.

'I'm leaving, Jason,' she repeated, determined not to back down – although her voice cracked, unable to believe she was saying all of this to him.

'At least let us give you a proper send off. We'll go for a few drinks and maybe we can stay in touch,' he said, his voice now full of desperation, and Karen had to admit she suffered a moment of hesitation, wondering whether she was making the right choice . . . before remembering her mother's words of warning: if she let him do it once, he'd do it again, no matter how good his intentions.

'I don't want a fuss. I've said goodbye to Bradley and I couldn't care less about Jessica,' Karen said, fighting the tears that were threatening to fall.

'What about me?' he asked.

'You know how I feel,' Karen said, keeping her eyes on him. Just a couple of weeks before, she had looked into his eyes and felt nothing but happiness. Now here she was, looking at him, saying her final goodbye. She never thought that day would come.

'Tell me what I have to do to make you stay,' he said.

'Nothing. My mind's made up,' Karen replied.

As she moved past her former boyfriend, starting to walk down the path that entered the housing estate, she had to bite her lip to stop her tears falling.

'One last try? Come on, I know you still love me,' Jason said, the pure desperation in his voice making Karen turn *around again. She could barely believe her eyes. He was on his knees in the middle of the pavement, as if he was literally begging for her to stay.*

'Walking away from you is one of the hardest things I think I'll ever have to do, but I need to do it,' Karen said, her voice reduced to nothing more than a whisper as tears threatened to escape her tired eyes.

'So you're gonna walk away from me right now and never come back?' he asked, his eyes full of tears.

'I'm staying with my cousin until I get myself sorted. I'll be fine, don't worry,' Karen said, pulling him up from the ground, wanting to spare him any more humiliation.

'I'm sorry,' he told her.

'I know,' Karen said, nodding weakly.

'Do I get one last hug?' he asked, unable to hold his emotions in any longer. A couple of rogue tears escaped and slid down his cheeks.

Karen had to give in. Seeing the look on his face, all she wanted was to comfort him, despite wanting to remain stony-faced about her decision to leave him and their life behind. She nodded her head gently and before she knew it, he'd wrapped his arms round her, pulling her as close as he possibly could. Karen couldn't deny she felt safe and comforted, the way she always used to feel when he held her, but now it was different. It was the final goodbye.

'I love you,' he said.

'I love you too. I always will,' Karen replied.

CHAPTER THIRTY
Present Day

Karen keeps her glance fixed on her car as she becomes lost in her thoughts. Bradley put his hand out flat in front of her face, snapping her out of it and she looks up at him, unsure of what he means.

'Give me your keys,' he says.

'No-one drives this beauty apart from me,' Karen says.

'I want to make sure you don't sneak off.'

'I won't,' Karen tells him – although the tight grip she has on her keys says otherwise.

'So hand over the keys,' he says, pushing his hand a little closer.

'Do I have to?' Karen asks, groaning.

'I've just driven across the city to see you all. I know it must be hard to be around Jess again, but it'd make me a very happy man if you could just put it to the back of your mind for this afternoon.'

'Fine, I'll stay. But only because I've missed you,' Karen says, placing her beloved car keys into Bradley's palm.

'I've missed you too.'

Ever the gentleman, Bradley holds out his arm and Karen accepts, resting her hand in the crease, allowing him to look after her. She offers him a grateful smile before they slowly make their way back to the steps that lead to Jessica's flat.

'So how have you been?' Karen asks, realising she's been rather selfish since reuniting with him, having asked nothing about him or his life.

'Could be better,' he replies with a heavy heart.

'Oh, I know that feeling so well,' Karen says, letting out a little sigh, almost matching his.

'I take it I'm not the only guy you've been missing?' he says.

'What?' Karen asks, shocked by how well Bradley could still read her.

'You're still in love with Jason.'

'How can you possibly know that?'

'I've got magic powers, don't you know?' Bradley jokes, trying to make her smile.

'You learn something new every day,' Karen giggles.

'Seriously though, if you didn't love him then things wouldn't be awkward between you and Jess, and I wouldn't have caught you doing a runner,' he says.

'I never could hide things from you, could I?' Karen says with a little smile.

'No, so don't try fobbing me off with a lie.'

'Okay, okay, I surrender. You sure you don't work for the police? You could get the most complex suspects to fess up,' Karen says before sighing once again, feeling like the weight of the world had just been dumped on her shoulders. 'Truth is, I never stopped loving Jason. God knows I've tried to get him out of my mind, but it's impossible. He's always there.'

'Does he know?' Bradley asks.

'Course he does. That man knows me better than I know myself.'

CHAPTER THIRTY-ONE
1997

Jessica sat on the sofa in Jason and Karen's apartment. She knew she shouldn't really be there. They all had keys cut to each other's flats and they'd always been allowed to just wander in and make themselves at home. They were like family. Only today was different. She'd betrayed Karen, tore her and Jason apart, and now this flat was a lonely, dull place to be.

She was pulled from her thoughts by Jason coming into the flat. He immediately turned on his heels when he saw Jessica. Deep down he knew he was as much to blame for his split from Karen, but every time he'd seen Jessica since, he'd been overwhelmed with anger, barely able to look at her.

'We need to talk about this,' Jessica said desperately.

Jessica rushed to Jason, trying to take his hand to stop him leaving, although he immediately snatched it back, as if allergic to her touch.

'There's only one person I want to speak to Jess and it isn't you,' Jason said.

'How can you be like this? Did what happen mean anything to you?' Jessica asked, her voice cracking, upset and hurt over the way Jason was reacting.

'Oh come on, it's not like we're madly in love, is it? I'm with Karen. I love her . . .'

'Funny way of showing it,' Jessica said sharply.

'We were a mistake,' Jason replied.

'I don't see it that way,' Jessica said.

Jason sighed heavily, storming across the room, wanting to get away from Jessica.

'What?' Jessica asked.

'You, acting like we've done nothing wrong!' Jason said, his words full of anger, glaring straight into Jessica's eyes, his vision blurred by tears. 'We've broken Karen's heart.'

'Jason, I'm sorry . . .' Jessica said quietly.

'W-while she was being told she'd lost our child, I-I was . . .' Jason stuttered, tears spilling from his eyes.

Jason slouched on the sofa, exhausted by everything that had happened, and Jessica sat beside him, although she was more timid, more reserved than she was just moments before, knowing she needed to tread carefully.

'You would have been amazing parents. It would have been the most loved little kid in the world,' Jessica said, her voice soft, wanting to offer him comfort, despite the fact she wished they were together.

'She,' Jason said.

'It was a girl?'

'Our little Amelia Rose.'

'That's a pretty name.'

'We chose it ages ago, but we agreed we'd keep it to ourselves. Something for us to share; our own little secret,' Jason said.

'And yet here you are spilling your guts to your bit on the side,' Karen said, standing in the doorway. She was disgusted just seeing Jason and Jessica in the same room as each other.

'Karen. I didn't know you were there,' Jason said, offering a polite smile – which she didn't return.

'Obviously,' Karen said bluntly.

'He's been telling me how much he loves you,' Jessica said, having had a sudden change of heart, wanting to make things right.

'I don't want to hear it, Jess. It's over, like I said. I don't do second best,' Karen replied.

'Is that what you think you are?' Jason asked, horrified.

'Why don't I give you two some space to talk?' Jessica suggested, making her way towards the door.

'I don't want to talk,' Karen said, barely able to look at Jessica.

'I know you're hurting, Karen, but I also know that you and Jason are made for each other. Don't let his stupid mistake with me get in the way of that. I just want you to be happy,' Jessica said.

Jessica had barely finished her sentence before the palm of Karen's hand hit her cheek, causing a burning pain and bringing tears to Jessica's eyes.

'You want me to be happy? **That** just made my week,' Karen said, almost hissing at Jessica, her words like a dagger in Jessica's heart. 'I heard you just now, begging Jason to talk about what happened between you. You're not sorry at all.'

CHAPTER THIRTY-TWO
Present Day

Rushing out of the front door, faster than she probably should in her condition, her feet graze the pavement as if she's unconsciously trying to trip herself up. Veronica squints as daylight hits her. It's not particularly sunny, but after spending the night holed up in a grotty flat, the windows boarded up with cardboard and the lights broken, the daylight is like a laser to her tired eyes.

She has no idea where she is or how she ended up here. Looking around the estate, nothing is familiar, not the music blaring from someone's car nor the faint smell of chip fat coming from the local takeaway. Her stomach rumbles. She can't remember the last time she ate. At one time, she'd set up "home" near a restaurant – although she made sure she wasn't seen. The last thing she'd wanted was to ruin the reputation of the business by camping outside their front door. Back then her only source of food was the scraps the waiters discarded in the outside bin. Trawling through the rubbish bags, the rotten aroma knocking her back, she'd never felt more ashamed of herself. She never thought she'd end up with a life like this.

A couple, perhaps in their mid-twenties, head towards Veronica, walking their dog. She immediately tenses up. She hates strangers. They either pass her by without a glance or terrorise her. This particular couple look her up and down before exchanging a disapproving look with one another, and simply walk away. She despises being this person. The one that people judge. The one people avoid, in fear of catching something.

As she breathes a sigh of relief, she's overpowered by a fierce coughing fit hammering hard against her chest. She notices the couple of strangers flinch slightly before picking up their pace, wanting to get as far from her as they possibly could. She doesn't blame them. She'd do the same if she could.

She tries to clear her throat with one final cough, a sour-tasting bile rushing up her throat and out of her mouth to land in a small puddle on the path in front of her. Just the sight of it makes her stomach turn. She has to get away from it, the reminder that she's not the free-spirited, lively girl she once was. Hearing the buzz of traffic, Veronica follows it, removing herself from the grimy estate where she had spent the night.

She's met with a blur of reds, blues, silvers and blacks as the cars whizz past, some people on their way to work, others just enjoying their lives. It brings her thoughts to her friends . . . her former friends. Veronica wonders what cars they drive. She wonders if they'll be in one of these cars driving past. It's wishful thinking, she knows, but when you live a life like hers, you cling to false hope like you completely depend on it.

Her legs ache terribly, feeling they could give way at any moment. She can feel her body slowly giving up just a little more with each passing day. Walking. One of the primary functions of a human being and she's struggling to do it. She can't even talk too much anymore, not without erupting into a coughing fit. Veronica wishes it wasn't like this but she has no choice. She has to live with what she's done. She has to suffer for it.

She stumbles, her face clashing with the harsh gravel. A few hours ago she wouldn't have been able to feel such pain, her body wrapped in a protective shield of strong drugs. Or maybe suffocated would be the better word. There's nothing safe or comforting about heroin. As she brings herself from the ground slightly, sitting upright on the path, her body begins to shake again: the familiar sign of withdrawal. Folding her arms across her chest, needing some warmth, the skin of one arm touches the cigarette wound on the other, sending a searing pain through every inch of her body.

Feeling tears in her eyes, she rubs them viciously. She shouldn't cry. She's got no right. Taking a deep breath, Veronica uses all the strength, although not a lot, to pull her body from the ground. She doesn't have a clue where she's going as she starts to walk again, or how far she's going to get, but she has to get away. She has to hide again.

With seconds, she steps on a stone, the hard rock pushing into the exposed part of the bottom of her foot, the sole of her shoe having worn away years ago. It's the final straw for her battered body and she finds herself falling to the ground once again. Feeling a sharp pain on her cheek, she reaches to feel it, blood seeping onto her fingers. Another injury to the list.

Veronica feels herself tense up again as one of the passing cars slows down and stops right beside her.

CHAPTER THIRTY-THREE
Present Day

They're talking. Or at least Bradley's talking. And Jason imagines Karen and Jess are throwing catty insults back and forth. It's such a mess. One friend missing, two at each other's throats, himself and Bradley trying to keep it all together. Not that Jason's much use right now.

A daughter. A fourteen-year-old daughter. Natalie. He never knew she existed. All the years that have gone by and he never knew he had a little girl. Ever since Karen lost their baby, he'd been hoping to become a father to a baby girl one day, but his ex-wife Amanda had given him two sons. He hadn't been disappointed. He loves them more than anything, but he'd still wanted a girl. Now he's got her.

CHAPTER THIRTY-FOUR
2003

Jason's life had gone downhill since leaving university. He'd never really wanted to be there in the first place, only applying to the uni so he could be near Karen. He couldn't be without her back then. Some things never changed.

He used to go out every weekend in the hope he'd bump into her out with her friends or even with a new guy. It wouldn't have put Jason off. He knew they had something special. Something neither of them would ever be able to recreate with another person. It might have been six years since they'd parted but he still loved her as much as he did back then and he'd have done anything to get her back. However, he knew that it was unlikely to happen. She'd probably be married to someone who really appreciated her, really knew how lucky they were. He should have known.

After getting a drink, Jason scanned the room. Then he saw her. Jessica. Stood at the end of the bar, on her own, concentrating on the bottom of her glass.

'You look amazing,' Jason said, standing behind her.

'I thought I told you I wasn't interested!' Jessica shouted, sounding frustrated, before turning around and locking eyes with him. Her face was a picture. 'Jason? Sorry I thought you were someone else.'

'I guessed as much. You been getting some hassle?' Jason asked, pulling himself up onto the stool beside her.

'Yeah, you know what lads are like,' she said, shaking her head. 'Sorry. Again. I'm talking like I'm out with Karen and Veronica. It's been so long you'd think I'd be over it by now.'

'No worries. It's true though. I bet every bloke in here is eyeing you up tonight,' Jason said, offering her a kind smile, trying not to focus too much on their absent friends.

'You think?' Jessica asked as a shy smile appeared on her face: she never knew how to take a compliment.

'I know,' Jason said as his eyes looked her up and down, admiring her outfit: a short, tight red dress that showed off her figure. 'I, in particular, am a sucker for a woman in a little red dress.'

Jessica didn't speak, although her eyes ran over Jason's body, admiring him in the way he'd just admired her, before their gaze met, locking intensely for a few moments.

'Drink?' Jason asked, flashing her a cheeky grin.

Karen used to love his grin, he remembered with a heavy heart.

CHAPTER THIRTY-FIVE
Present Day

It must have hurt Karen, Jason thought, when just a couple of hours ago she came face to face with his daughter. The daughter he shares with Jessica. She's right. She does have his eyes. His cheeky grin.

Still to this day, Jason doesn't know why he took Jess back to his place that night. She looked gorgeous in that red dress and of course they had a connection. After being friends for almost twenty years, you can't not have a connection. But she wasn't Karen. She'd never be Karen.

He never seems to know what he's got until it's gone. His relationship with Karen. His marriage to Amanda. His relationship with his sons. He lets people down time and time again, pushing his luck, hedging his bets, seeing if the grass really is greener.

It never is.

CHAPTER THIRTY-SIX
Six Months Ago

Sitting in his car, his hands resting on the steering wheel despite the engine being off, Jason watched as his ex-wife Amanda left their family home. Old family home. They're not a family anymore. Another of his mistakes.

Their two young sons, five-year-old cheeky and excitable twins, ran excitedly from the house and past their mother, their little legs carrying them down the steps. Jason had to laugh. Just like he was at their age.

'Boys, watch the road!' Amanda shouted before locking the front door, whilst also keeping an eye on the twins.

Hurrying down the steps, her attention turned to Jason, clearly angered by his presence. Eager to keep him from their children, she unlocked the car, putting the boys on the back seat and immediately closing the car door.

'I'm sure I told you to stay away,' she said, approaching the open window of Jason's car.

'You can't do this. I have rights,' Jason told her. It's hard to believe they were ever a happy family after such a bitter divorce.

'You gave up those rights the moment you went home with that cheap barmaid of yours,' she told him.

'I know I hurt you, but the boys shouldn't have to suffer. I'm their dad. It's only fair that I get some access to them,' Jason replied.

'They've barely noticed you're gone,' she said, although they both know that wasn't true.

'That's a lie. They're proper daddy's boys,' Jason said.

'No, they're not.' She shook her head.

'Look at them,' Jason said, turning her attention to their sons, who were now standing by Amanda's car waving at him. 'It looks like they know exactly who I am.'

'Get back in the car!' Amanda shouted over to the boys and her cheeks flushed a deep shade of red. Jason knew she was embarrassed.

'You used to tell anyone that would listen how great I was with the kids,' Jason reminded her.

'I was wrong. Just give it up, Jason,' she said.

'You'll be hearing from my solicitor,' Jason replied.

'I'm quaking in my boots,' she answered sarcastically, before storming back to her car, climbing in and speeding off down the road.

A wave of irritation soared through Jason's body as he witnessed this, the only reminder of his ex-wife and children was the screech of the tyres ringing in his ears and the musty smell of the engine lingering in his nostrils. Jason smacked his fist against the steering wheel, venting his frustration.

CHAPTER THIRTY-SEVEN
Present Day

He's staring into space, a frown etched on his forehead. He's not been listening to a word anyone has said, Karen can tell. The look on his face, she's seen it many times. When they were together, she'd be chatting away to him, sometimes for an hour at a time, and then she'd turn around to find him staring blankly ahead. He'd try and make out that he was just concentrating really hard on what she was saying, but she knew he'd never heard a word and that he was day-dreaming about the football, or about a night in town with Bradley sinking a few pints.

Karen used to find his little habit cute back then, but now it's just winding her up. He's not even stood near her. He stood with her. With Jessica.

'As nice as this reunion is, well, sort of . . .' Karen says, glaring at Jessica. She's watching Jason like a pathetic little kid with a crush. It's making her feel sick. 'Can we just get on with looking for Veronica?'

'Did she turn up last night?' Bradley asks.

'Yeah. She tried talking to me but I didn't react particularly well. She lashed out at me and then disappeared,' Karen tells him, wishing she'd gone after Veronica or at least said hello. It must have taken a lot for Veronica to approach her and all she did was stare at her like she was some sort of freak.

'Did she not leave a number?' Bradley asks, seeming a little disappointed.

'That would have been tricky, given she's homeless.' Karen says. 'I doubt she would have given me her number anyway, even if she had one. I barely gave her chance to explain her situation. I didn't ask anything about her.'

'A bit selfish, don't you think?' Jessica says, raising her eyebrows at Karen, as if mocking her.

'It was a shock. She doesn't even look like the same person,' Karen says, trying to defend herself, although the truth is she agrees with Jessica. She does feel selfish.

'Twenty years is a long time,' she replies.

'She's homeless,' Karen repeats.

'You keep saying that, but Veronica never actually said she was on the streets,' Jessica says.

'You didn't see the state of her.'

'No, because someone scared her off before I had the chance,' Jessica says, the tone of her voice making Karen's blood boil. She clenches her fists.

'Karen's right. She was a mess,' Jason says, suddenly joining the conversation, finally snapping out of his daze.

Jessica narrows her eyes at Jason, obviously annoyed that he was taking Karen's side over hers.

'The only thing left of the old Veronica was her tattoo,' Karen says, although she's turned her attention to Bradley, rather than Jessica.

'Alright, well she can't have gone far if she was on foot. Plus, if she's as bad as you say she is, she'll be lacking energy anyway. I'll take my car. Karen, you take yours. We'll go off in two's and just drive around,' Bradley explains, taking control of the situation. Karen's glad. If Jessica keeps going the way she is, she won't be responsible for her actions.

'And what if she's been hurt?' Karen asks, the very thought of her old friend being in any pain bringing a sadness to her heart.

'Whoever isn't driving can ring round the hospitals, see if they've had anyone taken in,' Bradley replies.

'We should ring the police as well,' Jason says.

'No!' Jessica exclaims, as if horrified by the notion of involving the police. 'No, it'll probably frighten her if she starts hearing police sirens chasing after her. We'll look for her first and then, if there's still no luck, maybe we'll report her.'

CHAPTER THIRTY-EIGHT
Present Day

Where is she?

A blur of colour. Blues and greens. Grey. Looking up, a rush of white. Bright white. Like a glowing line along the ceiling.

The soft mutter of voices vibrates Veronica's eardrums. She winces, the murmurs sending a shudder down her spine, her senses heightened in the cold wake of last night's storm. No-one seems to notice, continuing to go about their business, performing each test and task in no time at all. She looks around as her vision starts to focus a little better, her head pounding, and finds a drip hooked up to her arm.

Here she is again. Veronica never thought she'd be back in this place. She was doing pretty well until now. The last time she was here, she watched a family come to visit their mother. Or at least she thinks it was their mother. Could have been their sister, or even just a family friend, but she was around Veronica's age and it hit home: who'd visit her? How many people would call to find out visiting times for her?

None.

Veronica wanted to change. She wanted to stay out of hospital for good, or at least make sure she had people that would care about her if she were to end up being admitted again.

Looks like she failed.

CHAPTER THIRTY-NINE
Present Day

Driving through nearby housing estates and main roads, anxiously searching for their missing friend, Jason and Karen have barely exchanged a word. Karen knows he's been watching her though. Every time she checks the passenger side mirror their eyes meet for a brief moment.

'Still in a mood with me, I see,' Jason says, keeping his eyes fixed firmly on Karen, despite the fact she's refusing to look at him.

Karen doesn't want to talk to him. She doesn't want to have to face a conversation about the past. It's too much for her to deal with right now, so she turns up the volume, wanting to block out his voice, but he finds the dial and turns it back down.

'Jealousy doesn't suit you. You're better than this,' he tells her.

'This isn't about us. We're supposed to be looking for Veronica,' Karen says, keen to keep her focus on the road ahead.

'Maybe we can talk afterwards? About me and you,' he says.

'It's been twenty years since there was a "me and you",' Karen says, remaining stony-faced, although she secretly loves the way he still refers to them as a couple, as if they've always been together.

'Doesn't mean we can't still talk about it,' Jason replies.

'In your dreams, babe,' Karen says.

As much as it pains her to be so distant from her ex-boyfriend, she refuses to forgive him, even though it's all she really wants deep down. It would be a sign of weakness and Karen's not weak.

*****

Jessica's been watching Bradley for some time. He's driving them around, searching for Veronica. There's a look on his face. It's a little like confusion, but she suspects it's more than that. When they'd got into his car, a short time ago, he put his mobile phone into the glove compartment straight away, almost like it was part of a routine. It's ringing now. The fourth time since they'd set off.

She's looking at Bradley, waiting for him to pull over so he can answer it, or even ask her to answer for him, but he doesn't. He doesn't even flinch.

'So, what's the deal with you and the missus?' Jessica asks as the phone becomes silent.

'What do you mean?' he asks, frowning a little. He's not mentioned anything about his wife or his marriage since arriving at her flat.

'You've got a lot on your mind and your phone's been ringing constantly,' Jessica says.

'So?'

'You've ignored each one of those calls. That screams marriage troubles.'

'You would make a very good detective,' he tells her, letting out a little chuckle.

'I don't think I would.' Jessica shakes her head, her heart skipping a beat.

'Danielle's going through a hard time at the moment. She's a very complicated woman and I've got to admit, it's taking its toll. She gets jealous if I go out on my own. She needs to know where I am and what I'm doing every second of the day,' he says.

'Is that why you were a no-show last night?' Jessica asks. They'd all been just as disappointed as each other that Bradley was absent from the party.

'I did plan on coming to the party, even got in the taxi. Then Danielle texted and I had to turn around. As much as she winds me up, I know she only acts the way she does because she loves me. I wouldn't have enjoyed the party if I knew she was at home in tears,' he explains and Jessica can't help but smile. She knows how much it would have meant for him to be able to come and see them again, and he gave it all up to be there for his wife. Not many blokes would do that.

'I always knew you'd make a good husband.'

'She deserves to have someone look after her.'

'So what makes today different?'

'It's not just her constant phone calls that get to me,' he says, and just when Jessica thinks he might be about to open up to her, Bradley sighs loudly. 'It's a long story.'

'We've got time,' Jessica says, waiting for a while, watching her friend, anticipating him off-loading his troubles onto her.

'Thanks, but I don't want to burden you with my problems. I just wanted to see you all again, see if it'd cheer me up,' he says.

'And has it?'

'Apart from Veronica going AWOL, yeah, it's been great.'

'Still a lovely man, even after all this time. You're a one-off Mr Knight. An absolute star,' Jessica says, smiling at him.

He's the kind of bloke every woman dreams of meeting. She wishes she'd found someone like him, it would have saved her a lot of heartache.

'I'm glad you think so,' he smiles back. A lovely, kind smile.

'But if you do need to talk, about anything, then I just happen to be a really good listener,' Jessica says.

'I'll bear that in mind,' Bradley replies, glancing at Jessica.

She offers him a smile, which he returns, although it's half-hearted. Whatever his problems, it's clear that it's draining the life out of him.

CHAPTER FORTY
Two Months Ago

Standing outside the bathroom, there was nothing but silence. Danielle had gone in there about ten minutes ago, and Bradley was concerned that she hadn't yet returned.

'Babe, you alright in there?' Bradley asked, pressing his head against the door so his wife can hear him.

There was no response. No reply. No running water. No movement.

'Please talk to me. You're really starting to worry me now,' Bradley said, knocking the door.

He pressed his ear to the door, his heart thumping, knowing deep down what was wrong with his wife. It wasn't the first time they'd found themselves in this situation, but it didn't stop him worrying for her and feeling great pain at the haunting silence.

'Danielle, please unlock the door. Whatever's wrong, we can work through it together, alright? You know you never have to be afraid when I'm here,' Bradley told her, knowing she needed reassurance.

After a few moments, he heard Danielle on the other side of the door, releasing the lock. Bradley remained on the same spot, knowing she needed him close. She opened the door, black mascara-filled tears tattooed onto her cheeks and her pale skin blotchy.

Then he saw it. The white stick in her trembling hand.

Another negative pregnancy test.

Bradley was unsure of what to say, and he knew she felt the same as he pulled her close, allowing his broken wife to dissolve into tears once again.

CHAPTER FORTY-ONE
Present Day

They pull over in a lay-by, taking a break from their search. Bradley and Jessica have drawn a blank and the sinking feeling in the pit of their stomachs tells them there's only one place they need to check. Bradley takes his mobile from the glove compartment. It hasn't rung for some time and for a while he seemed calmer, a little more at ease.

'Damn! My battery's flat,' he says, throwing his mobile back into the glove compartment. 'Can I borrow your phone to call the hospital?'

'Yeah, course,' Jessica replies, grabbing her handbag from beside her feet.

She searches frantically for her mobile phone, which has fallen right to the bottom of her bag. Natalie always tells her she needs a smaller one. Perhaps she should listen to her occasionally. As she moves her hand around the bag, she knocks something out of it. Something she wants to keep hidden.

Jessica manages to stop it before it hits the seat and stuffs it back into her bag, but she knows Bradley is intrigued.

'What's that?' he asks, confused.

'Nothing,' Jessica says, but he's obviously not convinced. Catching sight of herself in the car window, she looks like a rabbit caught in headlights, her heart thumping so loud she can actually hear it.

'You okay?' he asks, obviously concerned by the sudden change in my mood.

'I thought we were in a hurry to find Veronica? Call the hospital and find out what's going on,' Jessica replies, perhaps a little too sharply as she passes him her mobile phone.

'Right, sure.'

Jessica breathes a sigh of relief as Bradley dials 999, pressing the mobile to his ear, and she wedges her handbag in between her leg and the car door. Secrets are supposed to be just that.

Secret.

CHAPTER FORTY-TWO
Present Day

Danielle is sitting on the sofa, occasionally sipping from a mug of tea. The TV is on – a home improvement show – but she isn't really watching it. Denise walks into the room; she looks tired and a little emotional, although she's trying to stay strong for her daughter. She perches on the arm of the sofa.

'What time is your appointment tomorrow? Denise asks.

'Half twelve,' Danielle replies, removing her eyes from the TV.

'Do you want me to come with you?' Denise offers.

'We're fine, just the two of us,' Danielle reassures her mother, although she senses she's gearing up for a lecture about Bradley.

'That's if Bradley even shows up,' Denise says, disapprovingly.

'Of course he will. He wants this as much as I do. This is the perfect time for me and Bradley. You'll see. It's going to make everything better,' Danielle says, smiling at Denise, who smiles back, although it's obvious she's not convinced.

There was only one thing that could heal this family, and they knew they'd never get it.

CHAPTER FORTY-THREE
1997

Work. Arguing with Danielle about exam revision. Housework. Dinner. A call from Brian to say he was going to work late. Just a normal day for Denise. A normal day. Right up until 10pm.

That knock at the door.

The two police officers stood in front of her, their hats in their hands, solemn expressions on their faces.

Denise's heart was racing so fast she thought it would burst straight out of her chest.

'Mrs Carter?' one of the police officers asked.

'Yes . . .' Denise said, her voice barely audible, her terror robbing her of her voice.

'May we come inside?' the police officer asked gently.

'S-say it . . . w-whatever it is . . . just s-say it,' Denise stammered.

'It's about your husband. Mr Brian Carter,' the second police officer told her.

'What about him? He's fine. He's probably just lost track of time at the university. It's his second home, that place,' Denise replied, trying to lighten the mood, ease her own worries.

'There's been an incident and Mr Carter-'

'Brian . . . please,' Denise said, desperate to stop them saying the word out loud. She knew what was coming.

'Brian was found an hour ago.'

'Found?' Denise whispered, her heart sinking, the whole world spinning around her. She clung to the stair banister.

'We're still investigating, but it looks like he was attacked, hit over the head. We're very sorry, Mrs Carter. . .' – the police officer explained, pausing, looking into Denise's eyes, seeing her terror, feeling her pain – '. . . Brian has passed away.'

Before the police officers could say anything more, Denise hit the ground, her body limp, as if her muscles had dissolved. Danielle, who was standing in the living room doorway, thought her mother had died from the shock, until she heard the most gut-wrenching, heart-breaking screams coming from her. She rushed to her mother's side, pulling her close, cradling her parent. It still hadn't sunk in what the police officers had said. Danielle's mind was a blur. But she was determined to be strong for her mother, make her father proud.

Proud of his little girl.

She'd always been his little girl.

CHAPTER FORTY-FOUR
Present Day

Bradley didn't think he'd ever been in such a tense atmosphere. He's not usually one to suffer from claustrophobia, but stood against the metal bar in this lift, he's counting the seconds, praying the doors will open. None of them are speaking, their minds focused on where they're are heading: Veronica's hospital bed.

When he got through to the hospital, Bradley was told that someone by the name of Veronica James had been admitted earlier that day. They wouldn't disclose the reason, but he didn't mind. He had the information they needed. After calling Jason, the four of them met in the car park downstairs. They exchanged smiles, pleased they'd tracked down their friend; but once they entered the lift, the mood soured.

Karen and Jessica are stood opposite one another; Karen beside Jason and Jessica beside Bradley. They're shooting looks at one another, and he can see Karen's jaw twitching, as she's obviously gritting her teeth in frustration. Bradley knows it's been hard for her, reuniting with Jessica and Jason, revisiting those old memories, tending to old wounds.

CHAPTER FORTY-FIVE
Present Day

Veronica hasn't got a clue what's going on. She's been sat in this bed, twiddling her thumbs, unsure of what to do with herself for what seems like hours. Her throat feels a little dry so she takes a sip of cooling water from beside her bed, preparing herself to call over a nurse once one becomes available.

The curtain has been closed around her bed. Perhaps she's bad for business. Odd really, when you think of all that these people must see, and yet people have to be shielded from a tramp. Seeing the curtain begin to twitch, Veronica clears her throat, ready to question the staff, but she doesn't get the chance. As the curtain opens she finds her former friends at the foot of her bed: Jason, Jessica, Karen and Bradley, they're all here. She blinks hard, convinced her mind is playing tricks on her, but they remain, looking at her, troubled expressions etched on their faces.

'What are you lot doing here?' Veronica asks, her voice husky from the dehydration.

'We were worried about you,' Jason says.

'I suppose they told you what a mess I am,' Veronica mutters, turning her attention to Bradley. He still looks the same as he did back then: handsome, kind, a real diamond of a man.

'We wouldn't gossip about you, Veronica. We're concerned, that's all,' Karen tells her, trying to reassure her.

'So, are y-you okay? Sorry, s-silly question,' Bradley asks, stumbling over his words.

'I haven't been okay for a long, long time,' Veronica says, bowing her head. She can't bear to look at them. She's too ashamed.

'We were talking earlier and we decided you should come and stay with me for a while,' Karen says.

'No, there's really no need,' Veronica says, shaking her head.

'You're homeless,' she tells her, as if she doesn't already know.

'You're all better off without me. I wouldn't want to intrude,' Veronica replies, finally looking up at her friends again. She's determined to protect them from the truth, from her.

'I've got a spare room, and there's a job with your name on it at my salon. It'll just be sweeping up and making tea, but it's better than nothing, right?' Karen says and Veronica can't help but feel guilty. After everything she's done, she's still got her friends trying to look out for her.

'I don't deserve-'

'Stop. I know you think you don't deserve our help, but it's not your fault you're on the streets. I'm not taking no for an answer.'

'I'm really grateful but . . . please just go.'

'No,' Jessica says firmly.

'You've developed a feisty streak since I last saw you.' Veronica rolls her eyes, unable to stop a little smirk appearing on her lips as she remembers the way they used to be.

'Friends don't walk out on each other,' Jessica says, and Veronica watches as her gaze falls on Karen. The atmosphere is tense between them and Karen refuses to look at her. God knows what's gone on there.

'I walked away from all of you twenty years ago,' Veronica says.

'But did you ever stop caring about us?' Bradley asks.

'No, course I didn't,' Veronica says. She's missed them every single day since she left; thought about them every single day.

'Well, we still care about you. We're not walking away,' Jason replies.

'You have my permission to leave. Don't worry, I won't make out like you're bad people. You don't have to feel guilty about it. Just go. Forget about the reunion,' Veronica says. As much as she appreciates their support, she's beginning to find it all a bit overwhelming. She knows they'd soon feel differently about her if they knew the truth.

'What's got into you, Veronica?' Jessica asks.

'Is someone after you?' Karen asks, frowning.

'What? No. Why would you think that?' Veronica asks, her heart thumping in her chest. She knows she must look guilty.

'Why are you trying to get rid of us?' she asks, not taking her eyes off Veronica.

'Because you're the best people I've ever known, and you deserve the best. I'll only hold you back. Please, I'm trying to help. Just leave,' Veronica pleads with them. She'd never forgive herself if she destroys their lives. She is definitely capable. But her friends deserve more; they deserve better.

'The doctor says you're free to go, so get your coat on and I'll drive you back to mine,' Karen tells her, taking control of the situation. 'Brad, will you be alright getting to mine? Jase can go with you and Jess, he knows the way. Pick up some pizza on your way, we need to fatten up the patient.'

Jessica glares at Karen. She obviously hates being told what to do, especially by Karen, although Veronica's not entirely sure why. The last time they were all together, at university, things were fine. Well, fine between her friends anyway. Veronica's not sure she's ever been fine. Karen and Jess had put their arms round each other, trying to offer comfort as she'd said her goodbyes. There was no bad feeling, no nasty glares, just friendship. She thought they'd be alright without her. That in twenty years' time they'd still be friends, still comforting one another, still tearing up the dance floor on a Saturday night. She couldn't have been more wrong by the looks of it.

As Jessica follows Bradley and Jason out of the cubicle she pushes past Karen, shoving into her arm so she loses her balance slightly. It's all rather childish, but Veronica can't think what could have happened to make a feud last quite as long as this. She didn't even apologise. Just walked off as if nothing had happened.

Karen seems a little hurt by what Jessica has just done, but instead of wallowing in self-pity she plasters a smile on her face. Veronica remains in bed, not really wanting to follow her orders. She feels overcome with guilt. She doesn't deserve their love and support. Like she told them before, she's better off alone.

'Come on, I won't tell you again. Get up and put your coat on,' Karen says, putting Veronica's coat on her lap and walking out of the cubicle, assuming she'll be right behind her. Veronica has to smile. She's always been the same. What Karen says, everyone else does. What Karen wants, Karen gets.

CHAPTER FORTY-SIX
Present Day

Sitting in the middle of the back seat of the car with Bradley driving and Jason in the passenger seat, Jessica's blood is literally boiling. They're chatting amongst themselves, but she can't make out what they're saying, she's too lost in her own thoughts. How dare Karen bark orders at them like that? If it was down to her, she'd have stayed at the hospital with Veronica, spoken to her for a bit longer, found out what *she* actually wanted. No chance of that when Queen Karen was swanning round.

Jessica folds her arms across her chest and turn her attention to the blur of traffic on the other side of the window.

'Are you gonna sit there with a face like a smacked backside all night?' Jason asks, turning in his seat so he's looking at Jessica.

'Where does Karen get off, bossing us around like that?' Jessica says.

'She's trying to help Veronica,' he replies.

'Stupid cow,' Jessica mutters under her breath, although it's loud enough for the guys to hear.

'It's what friends do. I'm sure she'd do the same for you,' Jason says, but Jessica can tell he's not particularly convinced by what he's saying.

'We both know that's not true,' Jessica tells him. 'And did you see the way she was with me and you back at mine? All those nasty little looks she was giving?'

'It must be really hard for her, after what happened,'

Bradley says, glancing in his rear-view mirror.

'So, I'm still the villain, yeah? Twenty years have gone by since then and she's still getting all the sympathy,' Jessica says, rolling her eyes.

'You two have got a daughter together. It was a shock for me to find out, so I can't imagine how much it's messed with her head,' Bradley replies, raising his eyebrows at Jessica in the mirror. She can tell he's disappointed but she won't let it get to her.

'Maybe she's realised that I had more of a connection with him than she ever did. Eh, Jase?' Jessica says, a small smirk creeping onto her lips.

'Stop it,' he warns her, his voice stern and unforgiving.

'Now you've turned against me? Honestly, what hold does that woman have on you?' Jessica asks, frustrated. She's always been on the side-lines.

'I love her,' he tells her.

'You didn't seem to love her much that night,' Jessica says, rolling her eyes again. It's childish, she knows, but that woman makes her blood boil.

'Stop, Jess, or you can get out of this car right now. I mean it,' Bradley replies, becoming the authority figure, just like he always was back then.

Despite Jessica's best efforts to stay unaffected by the warnings, she finds herself shrinking into her seat.

CHAPTER FORTY-SEVEN
Present Day

They'd arrived back at Karen's apartment around half an hour ago. Veronica had been telling Karen to stop the car or turn around pretty much all the way there, but she wouldn't listen. Surprise, surprise.

Within seconds of opening the front door, Karen had pushed her into the bathroom – a beautiful black and white bathroom, like something out of a Hollywood film. There were spotlights round the mirror, the lights reflecting off the little glittery specks on the wall tiles. Judging by the way Karen flinched when the lights came on, as if blinded, Veronica guesses it was not what she wanted.

Karen's told her little about her life, having been floored upon seeing her at the party yesterday; however, it's obvious she's unhappy. She never could hide how she really felt from her friends. That's what made their bond so special.

After letting Veronica shower, using all her posh, expensive-looking shower gel, shampoo and conditioner, Karen had picked out an outfit from her wardrobe. A black pair of skinny jeans and a beautiful blouse. Veronica didn't feel worthy of wearing such clothes. They looked far too good for someone like her, but the first touch of the soft, silky material was a welcome comfort in contrast to the harsh, ever-changing weather slapping her in the face.

Veronica barely recognised the refreshed feel of her hair. It's long, always has been, but it was normally out of control. Tangled, thick with grease, itchy. *Having a hairdresser as a mate has come in handy*, she thinks to herself, trying to calm her nerves.

*****

Turning the hairdryer off, filling the room with silence once again, Karen runs her fingers through Veronica's hair. It's much nicer than it was earlier today: no grease, no split ends and no bad roots. It's hardly her fault for letting her hairstyle go, but as a stylist, Karen can't stand to see hair neglected. Plus, Veronica deserves to be looked after.

Karen takes the mirror from the kitchen counter, the lights on the kitchen ceiling catching it, startling her like a bolt of lightning: when you exist in a world of monochrome, any glint of sparkle or colour shocks you. Holding the mirror in front of Veronica's face, her new reflection stares back. As well as sorting her hair out, Karen has applied some make-up. Nothing too heavy, just a glowing, natural style that brings out her eyes. They were always her best feature. They drew people in. She used to smile with her eyes. Karen wants her to be like that again.

In her salon, her favourite moments are just before the client leaves, when they admire her work for the first time, whether it be nails, hair or make-up. She loves the effect a new look can have on someone. They come in, feeling tired and a little run-down, bored with their dull, everyday routines, and they go out looking and feeling like a million dollars, ready to take on the whole world. It makes Karen's day.

She's experiencing that feeling now, watching Veronica as she admires her new appearance. For the first time in what Karen guesses to be years, she's looking just a little bit like the old Veronica. It's a relief.

'You're a hero,' Veronica tells her, taking a closer look at her reflection in the mirror.

'It's no big deal. I do this for a living,' Karen says, shrugging, not wanting to take anything away from Veronica's moment of glory.

'Not just for doing my hair and make-up. For everything. I'm pretty sure rescuing your messed-up mate isn't part of your job description,' she says.

'I wouldn't have been able to live with myself if I'd just walked away,' Karen says, running her fingers through Veronica's hair again. She wonders how long it's been since she had soft, silky hair.

'I don't think Jess is too happy,' Veronica says, shocking Karen. The old Veronica didn't care what people thought of her, whether people liked her or not. Now she's sat here, twiddling her thumbs, her shoulders hunched, like a scared little girl.

'That's not because of you. It's difficult for the two of us to be around each other,' Karen says, wanting to reassure her. Veronica's got enough on her plate right now without feeling guilty about something that's not even her fault.

'What happened?'

'We didn't exactly part on the best terms.'

'But why? Come on, you can tell me. It's not like I'll go blabbing to all my mates, is it?' she says and a wave of sadness hits Karen. She hates to think of her being all on her own.

'I found her in bed with Jason,' Karen says, a sharp pain soaring through her heart as she remembers that day. The second worst day of her entire life.

'Jess and Jason?! I never thought they'd do that to you,' she gasps, horrified.

'Me neither,' Karen says. 'I ended things with Jason and left uni for good. Last night was the first time I've seen either of them since that day.'

'And you still haven't forgiven them?'

'I want to, but it's hard. I was pregnant and . . .' Karen replies, although she finds her voice trailing off as she remembers the child she loved and lost. The child she shared with Jason.

'Pregnant?' Veronica says, turning around to look at her, making her hair fall free from Karen's hands.

'I found out just after you left. I did try calling, but I guess you changed your number or something.'

'Yeah.'

'I'd just come back from my scan when I caught them together. That's why it's so hard for me to forgive them. I'd just been told I'd lost our baby, and instead of being at the appointment, holding my hand, Jason was in our bed with Jess,' Karen tells her.

'I'm so sorry for your loss,' Veronica says, her eyes filling with tears.

'Me too. I've had another little girl since then, but it doesn't mean I don't miss the one I lost.'

'Of course not,' Veronica says, before glancing round the room. White walls, white floor, black furniture. No ornaments. No photos. 'Where is your daughter?'

'She goes to boarding school. She only comes home at Christmas and in the summer.'

'You must miss her.'

'If I'm honest, I never wanted her to go away. It was all Paul's idea,' Karen says, letting a little sigh escape from her lips. She doesn't care whether she has a genius kid or whether she's going to the best, most expensive school. Karen just wants her girl back home.

'Did he not want children?' she asks.

'He did, but he's a businessman. He always seems to be in competition with his workmates: who has the most beautiful wife; who has the smartest kid and the biggest, most amazing apartment. It's pathetic really. But anyway, what about you? Any family?' Karen asks Veronica, desperate to change the subject.

'No husband to speak of, thank goodness. I do have a son though: Jayden. He doesn't live with me. Obviously. The streets aren't safe enough for me, let alone a kid. Well, he's not really a kid anymore but . . .' Veronica says, talking as quickly as she can and then stopping. Perhaps she's scared. Or ashamed.

'How old is he?'

'He'll be twenty now.'

'You haven't been on the streets that long have you?'

'Apart from a couple of stints in rehab, I've pretty much been on the streets since I left uni. I mean, I had a flat to start with, but it all started to go wrong a couple of months down the line,' Veronica tells Karen, gradually feeling more at ease in her company, allowing herself to open up.

'What about Jenny? I mean, she's your sister,' Karen says.

'Golden Girl gave up on me a long time ago. So did my parents. So much for unconditional love, eh?' Veronica sighs.

It's no surprise to Karen that she isn't in contact with her family. They were never close. Veronica was always the odd one out. She chose nights out over nights in revising, and she had a habit of speaking before thinking.

'What happened after you left? Why did it all go so wrong for you?' Karen asks, unable to comprehend how someone's life could go downhill so quickly.

'Drugs. I'm clean now though. Well, I was clean until last night. That's why I ended up in hospital this morning,' she admits.

They reside in silence for a while. Karen can't speak. She knew she'd had a hard life. Veronica's appearance and nervous manner told her that within the first couple of seconds of reuniting, but to hear the truth, to hear the extent of her troubles from her lips, has shocked Karen to the very core.

The sound of the doorbell interrupts them, making Veronica flinch.

'It's alright. That'll be the others,' Karen says, breaking the silence and making her way to the door, plastering a smile on her face as she opens it to her friends. 'Come in.'

CHAPTER FORTY-EIGHT
1997

Jason, Karen, Jessica, Bradley and Veronica were all gathered in the living area of Karen and Jason's flat. It was Veronica's birthday, and 21st birthday balloons were hanging from the ceiling and some opened presents were on the coffee table. They were all dressed for a night out, but Veronica had made extra effort for her special night. She was humming along to the radio as she poured herself another glass of wine.

'Where's your new man?' Jessica asked, watching Veronica.

'Dumped him. He wasn't right for me,' Veronica said casually.

'Yeah, but she only dumped him after he'd handed over her presents,' Karen told the rest of the group with a smirk.

'Seriously? Veronica, what are you like?!' Bradley said, although he couldn't help but laugh. This was typical Veronica.

'What did he get you?' Jessica asked.

'The usual. Flowers, chocolates, wine,' Veronica replied.

'You could have bought all that down the local shop. Did you really need him to hand over the presents? The poor bloke. He was properly smitten with you,' Bradley said, shaking his head in amusement.

'He got me this dress too,' Veronica told them, striking a pose in her outfit, making her friends laugh.

'Ah okay, now I see why you did it. That dress is gorgeous,' Jessica said.

'Especially with a figure like yours, Veronica,' Karen said, despite being stunning herself, with a figure that most girls had to work hard to maintain.

'I'm sure you'll be finding a replacement for Harry tonight,' Jessica said, exchanging a grin with Veronica.

'That's the plan. It is my birthday after all,' Veronica replied, before going over to the mirror hanging on the wall, admiring her appearance. 'Do I need more mascara?'

'You're gorgeous. You don't even need make-up, you lucky thing,' Karen told her.

'Neither do you,' Jason said, putting his arm round Karen, pulling her in for a kiss.

'Give it a rest love birds! Now, where's my birthday cake?' Veronica said, sitting on the floor, waiting at the coffee table like an excitable kid.

'Give me two minutes,' Bradley said, hurrying into the kitchen.

Veronica picked up the Polaroid camera and took a photo of Karen and Jason. They smile for the first one, but Jessica playfully "photo-bombed" the second, making the others laugh.

'Pass me that,' Karen said, taking the camera from Veronica and pointing it at her. 'Smile for the camera, birthday girl!'

Veronica flashed a cheesy grin at the camera and Karen took a photo, just as Bradley walked into the room carrying a birthday cake with lit candles on the top. Veronica moved her presents from the coffee table and, as Bradley put the cake in front of her, they all sang Happy Birthday. When they'd finished, Veronica blew out the candles.

'Come on then, let's stuff our faces with cake, down some booze, and hit the clubs,' Veronica said excitedly, grabbing herself a massive slice of cake with one hand and picking up her glass of wine with the other.

'Why do I get the feeling we're gonna be carrying her home later?' Jessica said to Karen, raising her eyebrows.

'What's new?' Karen replied, laughing.

CHAPTER FORTY-NINE
Present Day

Reclining in the plush, sofa leather sofa, Bradley feels content. Really content. For the first time in years. They used to do this all the time when they were young. Maybe not in a penthouse apartment with millions of pounds-worth of furniture and gadgets surrounding them, but they used to gather in one of their living rooms, spending the evening sipping beers and chatting about whatever rubbish came into their heads. It was simple and it was fairly uneventful but they loved it all the same.

Bradley glances at each of his friends. Jessica on the floor, her phone pressed to her ear, answering another angry call from her daughter. Jason's daughter. Veronica is sat with her back to most of them, leaning against the glass coffee table, staring aimlessly at the blank TV screen. She's barely said a word since they arrived a couple of hours ago.

Karen is fussing round everyone, putting coasters under their drinks and laying sheets of kitchen towel on the floor and the bare surfaces as if trying to protect it from the pizza grease. Jason is sitting on the seat beside Bradley on the sofa, watching Karen's every move. His feelings clearly haven't faded. The way he's looking at her, you can't fake something like that and you certainly can't disguise it.

'Alright, alright, I'm coming home now. I'll get a taxi,' Jessica says down the phone, frustrated as she hangs up.

'I'll drive you, Jess,' Bradley offers.

'Are you sure?' Jessica asks.

'Yeah. I better be making tracks myself or I'll be in the doghouse for the next couple of weeks,' he replies, sighing a little. He really doesn't want to leave.

'Are you going?' Karen asks Jessica, suddenly coming out of the kitchen area, having missed the beginning of the conversation.

'Yeah.'

'Good,' Karen says bluntly, before standing a little closer to Bradley, offering him a friendly smile. 'You should stay a bit longer though, Brad.'

'I wish I could, but you know what it's like, responsibilities and all that,' Bradley tells her.

'Keep in touch, yeah?' she says.

'You try stopping me,' Bradley reassures her, kissing her on the cheek before turning to the others. 'Bye, guys.'

'See ya, buddy. Good seeing you again,' Jason says, offering his hand.

'And you,' Bradley replies, turning his attention to their silent friend, still sitting on the floor. 'Bye, Veronica.'

Bradley waits for a response but she remains silent, turning only briefly to give him a blank stare. When they were younger, she hated saying goodbye to them and she'd make a huge deal out of it, hugging each one of them so tightly they could barely breathe, kissing them on the cheek and waving like an excitable child until they were out of sight.

Now all they get is a blank, emotionless stare. There's something not right with Veronica, but he decides not to question her. He doesn't think she's got the strength for an interrogation, so instead, Bradley and Jessica leave Karen's apartment.

*****

The apartment goes quiet as soon as the front door closes and, for a few moments, they exist in an uncomfortable silence. It's strange. They used to spend almost every minute of every day together when they were teenagers and now here they are, unsure of what to say to one another. Karen never thought it would be like this.

Jason finishes his beer, putting the empty can on the table. He doesn't take long to down a drink, so there is still a coating of condensation on the outside of the can and it leaves a mark on the glass table. Karen finds her eyes drawn to it and before she can stop herself, she rushes over and places the can on a nearby coaster.

Jason looks at Karen, seeming a little worried by his actions, but she smiles softly at him, not wanting him to feel bad. It's not his fault she's like this. She never used to be.

'I suppose I should phone for a taxi too,' Jason says.

'You don't have to,' Karen says, surprising herself a little.

'What?' Jason asks, taken back by her statement.

'Well, I m-mean . . . you could have another drink . . .if you want?' Karen stutters, feeling embarrassed about the effect he has on her. She despises Jessica for acting like a love-struck teenager, and yet here she is, being exactly the same. She's a hypocrite, she knows that.

'I'd love to, thanks,' he says, a beaming smile appearing on his face. Karen smiles back.

'Help yourself,' Karen replies.

Jason walks past her, going into the kitchen, his arm brushing her as he passes. A shiver ripples through her body and her breath is taken for a moment.

Once he is out of sight, she makes her way to the radio, stored neatly in the small cupboard at the side of the sofa. It sits behind a glass door and, of course, the radio is monochrome to match every other lifeless, staid object in the apartment. Turning up the volume, it crackles slightly before a reporter's voice fills the room.

"... *floral tributes have been left outside the gates of the university, where Mr Brian Carter sadly lost his life exactly twenty years ago. His killer ...*"

Karen turns it off, cutting the reporter short. Veronica is still sitting on the floor in silence, her shoulders raised and hunched over. It was a terrible time for everyone at the university. It turned their worlds upside down.

'Hard to believe it's been that long already,' Karen sighs.

'I should go,' Veronica says, quickly getting up from the floor. Too quickly, given how fragile she still is.

'Where?' Karen asks.

'Anywhere,' she says. Her eyes are squinted slightly and she pushes her hand against the wall. Karen imagines she's dizzy, although being as stubborn as normal, is putting on a brave face.

'Don't be daft. I've told you the spare room is yours,' Karen says.

'I don't need it. I'll be okay,' she says, shaking her head.

'You'll be dead within weeks if you go back on the streets. Sit back down,' Karen tells her, much more firmly than before. She needs tough love.

'I might go to bed then,' Veronica says, relenting. She just needs to get out of the room.

'Okay. Well, it's all set up for you. Just make yourself at home,' Karen replies.

*****

Jason hears the door to the spare room open and close and a few moments later Karen joins him in the kitchen. He offers her a can, but as he suspected she would, she declines, taking a half-empty bottle of wine from the fridge.

'You can stay the night, if you want?' Karen offers.

'I'd love to,' Jason says, enthusiastically.

Jason can't take his eyes off her. After the day they've had, she still looks so glamorous, her make-up firmly in place and her hair styled perfectly. He wouldn't mind, of course, if she'd removed every scrap of make-up and pulled her hair into a ponytail. She's looks beautiful all the time. He'd tell her, but he knows she won't believe him. Paul's made sure of that.

Karen runs her eyes over Jason's face, occasionally letting her gaze fall on his lips before travelling back up to his eyes again. He's been trying to control the way he feels all day, but now it's just the two of them in the room he can't deny it anymore. Leaning into Karen, he makes his move, and to his surprise, she responds. It's only a few moments, however, before she does what she always does. She pulls away.

'Don't get your hopes up. You're on the sofa again,' she tells him before, pouring herself another glass of wine.

CHAPTER FIFTY
Present Day

It's 7.00am and Karen's been up and dressed for work for the last hour. She's never normally this organised in the morning, never waking before the shrill call of the alarm clock, but she's had a restless night. Lying in bed, her mind was racing with thoughts of the past couple of days: her friends, the reunion party, Paul . . . Jason. Knowing he was just the other side of the bedroom door, sleeping on the sofa, stopped her getting a wink of sleep. She wanted to go to him, to take him back to her bed, but something stopped her: fear.

They've been talking to one another for the last few minutes while Jason makes himself at home preparing breakfast. Karen likes the way it feels, having a man around the place to take care of her. It was like that with Paul for the first couple of years, then it went downhill. Jason's enjoying it too, whistling away while he cooks a fry-up.

Karen checks her watch again before glancing at the door to the spare room. Amelia's room. Veronica hasn't woken up yet. It's still early, but there's an uneasy feeling deep down that forces her to go and check on her friend. Going into the room, Karen crouches down beside the bed, watching Veronica sleep for a few moments, wondering when she'd last slept, had last been in a proper bed.

'Veronica . . .Veronica, wake up,' Karen says, shaking Veronica's body gently. She's scared to shake her too hard in case she hurts her. She's so fragile.

Veronica stirs, waking slowly from her sleep. She stretches her arms out either side of her, showing off her faded daisy chain tattoo once more, before sitting up in bed. Karen can tell it's taking all her strength. She's a little breathless and she rubs her eyes, smearing her mascara. Karen looks at the bedside table, seeing two empty cans of beer. She's probably hungover. It's not a lot of alcohol, but for someone so underweight and malnourished, two cans go straight to the head.

'What are you playing at? I gave you fruit juice,' Karen says. She must have crept into the kitchen in the middle of the night.

'Needed something stronger,' Veronica mumbles, holding her head in her hands.

'You shouldn't do that,' Karen tells her. Veronica had told her about her drug problem last night when she'd gone in to check on her, but Karen senses there's more to it. If she was addicted to one, she was probably addicted to the other. She knows it's not always the case, but she's sure twenty years on the streets would drive anyone to drink. When they can get their hands on it, of course.

'I only had it to help me sleep. You must understand that,' Veronica says, admitting her troubles to her.

'Breakfast and a shower, I think. I'll sort one of my outfits for you,' Karen says.

'Are you sure?' Veronica asks, moving herself to the end of the bed, her stick-thin, bruised legs hanging over the edge.

'I know my clothes are a bit baggy on you, but your own clothes literally disintegrated in the washing machine. Come on, take my arm,' Karen says, knowing that despite a night's sleep, she'll still be very weak.

*****

The sound of the bacon sizzling fills Jason's ears until he hears the bedroom door open. Turning around, he sees Karen slowly leading Veronica from the spare room, as if she's an elderly woman. It shocks him. They've been with Veronica for the past couple of days, on and off, but standing back and watching her, Jason realises just how much she's suffering.

'Morning, Veronica. What do you want for breakfast?' Jason asks, keen to help Karen care for their friend in any way he can.

'Nothing,' Veronica mutters.

'And by that she means a big fry-up,' Karen tells Jason.

'I don't do breakfast,' Veronica says, shaking her head.

'But that's only because you've had no other option. While you're under my roof, you're eating breakfast,' Karen says, like a teacher to a small child, and Jason can't help but smile as she guides their friend into the main bedroom and bathroom so she can shower. Her caring nature is one of her best qualities.

*****

Freshly showered and wearing another of Karen's outfits – a navy-blue blouse which hangs from her body like she's a human coat hanger and a pair of black trousers that drown her legs – Veronica's at the kitchen table, an empty plate and mug in front of her. She'd devoured her breakfast and been given seconds, along with three mugs of strong coffee. Karen and Jason have been so good to her, picking her up and giving her strength. After so many years running on empty, she feels at peace, with a full stomach and the care of her friends. That is, until they next put the radio on and she trembles, reverting back to that scared young girl again, and she startles when Karen starts talking.

'You're going to Jess's flat today,' Karen tells her.

'Why? I thought I could stay here,' Veronica says.

'There's a chance Paul might be home today. I can't risk you being here. Trust me, it'll be better if we all face him together,' Karen replies.

'Where are you going?' she asks.

'Work. I've got to let my team know we're getting a new employee on Monday,' Karen says, smiling excitedly at Veronica. She seems really keen for her to get started in the salon. It's like she thinks they'll become the latest "dream team": Veronica James and Karen Gallagher against the rest of the world.

'Yeah . . .' Veronica mutters, unable to say anything more. Something tells her she won't be starting her new job anytime soon, no matter how optimistic Karen is.

'And I've got to go and make sure my bar's still standing. I've not really bothered with it since the party,' Jason says.

'Do I have to stay at Jess's all night too?' Veronica asks, turning to Karen.

'No, she's going to bring you home about five. I'll be home by then,' Karen says.

'It'll be nice for you to have a change of scenery,' Jason tells Veronica; but he can tell she's not so sure.

'Yeah, why do you think I love my salon so much? It gets me out of this place,' Karen says, letting out a small laugh. She's not joking though. She hates this place, every single bit of it. Veronica can tell by the way she acts. She's like a stranger in her own home.

169

'Okay,' Veronica says, reluctantly agreeing to their suggestion.

'Good, she'll be here in ten minutes,' Karen replies, going to fetch Veronica's new shoes. Her trainers, along with her clothes, were in shreds in the bin and Karen had sent Jason on a last-minute dash to the shops to buy her a new pair.

CHAPTER FIFTY-ONE
Present Day

Dressed in his smart work clothing, his ID badge round his neck, Bradley goes into the kitchen. The cold kettle tells him he's in the doghouse. Danielle normally makes him a coffee every morning, without fail, along with a healthy breakfast to set him up for the day; instead, she is sitting at the kitchen table, a face like thunder and no breakfast in sight.

'You were home late last night,' she says.

'I tried not to wake you,' Bradley says, flicking on the kettle and fetching a mug from the cupboard.

'I didn't sleep much anyway. Especially with you out God knows where,' Danielle replies, the anger in her voice seeping through.

'I've already apologised,' Bradley says, sighing.

'I know. I wasn't having a go,' Danielle replies, suddenly calming down again. It's always like this. Her mood changes like the weather. Up one minute, down the next. Bradley just has to go with it.

'Could've fooled me.'

'Can I ask you something?'

'Course you can.'

'Have you got another woman?'

'What?' Bradley asks, taken back by her suggestion. It's not the first time, but it has been some time since she last asked him that question. She should know by now that he'd never betray her.

'You lied about going to work yesterday. Why would you do that if you didn't have something to hide?' she asks, her eyes narrowed in suspicion.

'There's no-one else for me, you know that,' Bradley tells her.

'Doesn't feel like it sometimes,' Danielle says, knowing she can pull at his heartstrings.

'I was with my friends,' Bradley says, realising it's just easier to tell her the truth.

'The ones from the party?'

'Yeah. I felt bad for missing the party, and I didn't want them thinking I didn't care, so I tracked Jessica down and paid her a visit. Karen and Jason were there as well,' Bradley replies.

'Why didn't you tell me?' she asks, hurt.

'I wanted to see how it went first. It could have been a disaster.'

'And was it?'

'No, it was brilliant. I didn't want to leave them, if I'm honest,' Bradley tells her, feeling a smile creep onto his lips.

'So, you'll be seeing them again?' she asks, sounding worried at the prospect.

'I'm hoping to pay them another visit later, after our appointment,' Bradley says.

'Can I come?' Danielle asks.

'Not today.' Bradley shakes his head, although he soon realises she's taken offense to this. 'But I'll speak to them today, see if they want to come round at the weekend. I'll meet you at the hospital at lunchtime.'

Bradley drops a kiss onto Danielle's cheek, hoping it will offer her some reassurance, before heading for the front door, picking up his briefcase at the foot of the stairs, deciding he'll grab some breakfast on the way into work.

CHAPTER FIFTY-TWO
Present Day

Jessica watches Veronica sitting on the sofa, her eyes fixed on the blank TV screen. It was similar to the way she had behaved at Karen's place the previous night and it put Jessica on edge. As much as she wants to help, there's something about Veronica that she just can't put her finger on. She can't work her out and this was a new one for Jessica.

'Can I get you another cup of coffee?' Jessica asks, desperate to get a conversation going with her friend. She knew she'd opened up to Karen, so why wouldn't she open up to the rest of them?

'No, thanks. I'll be bouncing off the walls,' Veronica says, shaking her head, barely taking her eyes off the TV.

'I guess it's been a while since you last had coffee, eh?' Jessica replies.

'It's been a while since I had most things,' Veronica says, the sadness returning to her voice.

Jessica's lost for words. She doesn't know how to comfort Veronica, how to make things right, and she'd hate to push her too far. If Veronica does another disappearing act, that really would make things worse between her and Karen and, right now, she didn't need that kind of drama. Despite everything, Jessica wanted them all to get back to how they were. Even if it took them years.

Sitting down at the small dining table, Jessica pulls yesterday's newspaper towards her. She's not had a chance to read it yet. It brings back memories. Bad memories. Awful. It was hard for them all, and it marked the beginning of the end of their friendship back then.

Looking at the main article, Jessica's heart sinks: Mr Carter. His murder. Front page news. The headline in big, bold letters, making it impossible to ignore.

'I still can't get my head around the fact it's been twenty years,' Jessica says. 'His poor family. All these years and still no justice. It's not right, is it?'

Jessica turns around, hoping for a response from Veronica, but she remains silent, still staring at the TV screen.

CHAPTER FIFTY-THREE
1996

The lecture room slowly emptied out after class, everyone ready to finish for the day. Everyone except Karen that was. She was still at her desk, finishing some notes when Veronica walked into the room and over to her friend.

'Anyone would think you live in this classroom, the amount of time you spend in here.' Veronica said.

'It's called getting an education. It's the reason we're here, after all,' Karen replied, trying to remain focused on her work; she had ambition, she wanted to work hard and prove herself.

'Teacher's pet,' Veronica says, nudging Karen, giggling.

'Says you. Jason told me you're a proper show off in Mr Carter's class. When you decide to turn up, that is,' Karen said, smirking.

'Can't help it if I'm his favourite, can I?' Veronica grinned childishly at her friend.

Brian Carter walked in, carrying a pile of textbooks. He smiled at Karen and Veronica, and went straight to the front of the lecture room.

'Oh, hi, Mr Carter. How are you?' Karen asked.

'Very well. And yourself?' Brian replied.

'I'm fine. Just got this one here telling me I spend too much time studying,' Karen said with a smile.

'I'm surprised you remember what a lecture room looks like, Veronica,' Brian joked.

Veronica had this effect on most of the lecturers. They knew she was cheeky and a bit of a trouble-maker, but they also knew she had a heart of gold, meaning they often let her get away with more than most students.

'Very funny, sir. You ever thought about stand-up?' Veronica replied.

Brian smiled, shaking his head in amusement at Veronica. Karen finished her notes and shoved her books into her bag, interrupting the eye contact between her friend and the teacher.

'Come on, let's go and meet the others,' Karen says, linking arms with Veronica as they head for the door.

Before leaving the room, Veronica glanced over her shoulder and playfully winked at Brian. It was an innocent gesture from Veronica, but to Brian, it signalled something more.

CHAPTER FIFTY-FOUR
Present Day

Unable to take the silence much longer, Jessica sits down beside Veronica, as close as her friend will let her get. She pauses for a few moments, looking at the framed photo that now sits on the side table – a group shot taken on a "Tequila Tuesday", just the five of them in a pub garden, surrounded by empty glasses with tipsy smiles on their faces.

'Do you remember much about our university days?' Jessica says, turning her attention back to Veronica, whose eyes still haven't moved from the blank TV screen.

'Bits. I've taken so many drugs over the years I'm surprised I can remember anything at all,' Veronica replies, frightening Jessica with her blunt honesty.

'You just try and cling on to the good times, I suppose?' Jessica says, trying to create a more positive atmosphere; perhaps this might help Veronica recover more quickly, rather than going over the same things with each person she speaks to.

'Yeah, I guess so,' Veronica replies, offering Jessica nothing but a split-second of eye contact.

'Can I–'

'I still don't want a coffee,' Veronica says, interrupting her friend. 'Something stronger might be nice. If you've got it?'

CHAPTER FIFTY-FIVE
1997

It was late and the lecture room was empty. It was just the two of them. The atmosphere had been good, the two of them joking around like they always did. This time didn't seem any different to Veronica. Until his hand landed on her knee. She thought it was an accident at first, but Brian didn't seem to be in any rush to move it. Instead his fingers began to caress her skin, his hand slowly making its way higher up her leg until it was nearing the hem of her skirt.

Veronica didn't know what was happening or why. She only ever wanted to joke around with Brian. It made the days pass more quickly if there was laughter. She never meant anything by it. He was a middle-aged man, and not bad looking for a man twice Veronica's age, but certainly not her type. Feeling a tug at her skirt, Veronica stood up, breaking free from his advances.

She dashed to the door, desperate to leave, but as she reached it, so did Brian. He reached out in front of Veronica and pressed his hand on the door, keeping it firmly shut. Veronica wanted to run away, scream, shout, climb out of the window, anything, but she was frozen, and her body completely shut down with fear as Brian leant in towards her. She could feel his breath, tainted with the stale stench of cigarette smoke, on her skin.

She tried once again to scream but Brian clamped his palm against her mouth, silencing her.

'Come on, I thought this was what you wanted. You're always messing around in my lessons, wearing clothes that are inappropriate for class . . . why else would you do that if you

didn't want me to touch you, kiss you?' Brian said, the tone of his voice changing to something Veronica had never heard before. She never thought he could be like this. He always seemed so normal. So nice.

His lips pressed against Veronica's neck. She felt dirty. Ashamed. But as his hand snaked up her leg and under her skirt, Veronica somehow found strength. She kneed him hard in the groin and he fell to the ground, groaning in pain.

Veronica grabbed the door and almost managed to open it when she felt Brian's hands on her hips. Trembling, terrified that she wouldn't make it out of the room, she once again used all the strength she could manage to shove him away from her.

There was a loud thud, and then silence.

After a few moments, Veronica plucked up the courage to turn around, and her knees almost gave way at the sight before her. Brian was lying unconscious on the immaculate white floor, scarlet blood seeping from the wound in his head, surrounding his ashen face, staining the collar of his shirt, scruffy and untucked from his trousers.

CHAPTER FIFTY-SIX
Present Day

Like a wild animal, Veronica snatches the tumbler from Jessica's grasp and as their hands meet for a moment, Jessica recoils. The bones in Veronica's hand jut out of her almost-transparent skin like the tip of a sharp knife and she feels as though she's been cut. Devouring every last drop of whisky in a matter of seconds, Veronica gazes longingly at the bottle. Jessica gestures for her to help herself and she does, pouring herself a rather generous amount. The alcohol could perhaps thaw Veronica's ice-cold mood, if nothing else.

Jessica doesn't normally let people drink in her home but she'd decides to break her rule just this once, seeing as it is one of the only things Veronica has spoken about. She hopes it will encourage Veronica to open up.

'One of those weeks, eh?' Jessica says, trying to lift the metaphorical gloomy cloud hanging over their heads.

'One of those lives more like,' Veronica says, or at least Jessica thinks that's what she says. With her chapped lips pressed against the glass and her nose resting on the rim, inhaling the alcoholic fumes, she is barely audible.

'What happened to you?'

'If one more person asks me that . . .'

'You'll tell the truth?'

Jessica can understand why Veronica is frustrated. They've bombarded her with questions ever since the reunion, but Jessica, for one, won't give up. With Karen out of the way, she can finally have a proper talk with Veronica. She's got a feeling that this runs far deeper than she'd like to admit. The truth so well-hidden amongst her lies, that upon first glance it appears it can never be discovered.

'It's nothing. I'm on the streets, that's all,' Veronica shrugs, as if her situation is entirely normal.

'Something must have put you there,' Jessica says.

'Financial difficulties. You know what I was like with all that stuff,' Veronica replies.

Her eyes drop to the floor for a moment before locking with Jessica's again. Then she does it. Laughs. Not real laughter, just an uneasy giggle. She does it so quietly that to an untrained ear it might sound like nothing more than a heavy breath, but Jessica knows her better than that.

She's nervous. Scared.

She's lying.

'Yeah, brilliant,' Jessica narrow her eyes, not believing a word Veronica says. 'You might have been a bit wild back then, but when it came to important stuff, you were always the most sensible.'

'That was twenty years ago. Things change. People change.'

'Not as much as this. Look at you,' Jessica gasps. She doesn't mean to but she can't help it. Her friend's transformation is breath-taking in the worst possible way.

Her baby-blue eyes once reflected her personality, glistening with vibrancy and mischief, but now they are dark. Really dark. In fact, it appears every trace of blue has disappeared, leaving her eyes a dull, murky grey, like a polluted ocean.

Veronica shifts uncomfortably in her seat, insecure in Jessica's gaze, as her attention turns to Veronica's hair. She used

181

to be so jealous of her gorgeous blonde hair, sparkling in the light as if encrusted with diamonds. Her locks flowed all the way down her back while Jessica's refused to grow beyond her jawline. Now Veronica's hair, despite being treated by Karen the previous evening, was looking unloved again. It was as though it had become so used to being dull and limp that it naturally went back to being that way after a short space of time.

Jessica has nothing to be envious of anymore. This is the hollow shell of her former friend.

Veronica coughs, bringing Jessica from her thoughts, and she looks at her, broken-hearted, like she'd projected them out loud.

'So, I'm not beautiful, get over it. We can't all be lucky like you and Karen,' Veronica rants, becoming so worked up she erupts into a debilitating coughing fit.

'You should get that checked,' Jessica says, alarmed by the vicious cough hammering on her chest.

'No!' she refuses. Still as stubborn as ever.

'It sounds nasty,' Jessica says, but she doesn't budge. She tries to take her arm but Veronica pulls away from her, wincing in pain as she does so. 'I'll take you to the hospital.'

'I said no.'

'You could be seriously ill.'

'So? It'd be best for everyone if I died,' Veronica says, her harsh words slaying Jessica like a lethal weapon.

'What happened to you?' Jessica asks again, her body shaking as shockwaves shoot through her being.

'If you ask me that one more time I swear I won't be responsible for my actions!' Veronica shouts, threatening her, her decaying teeth gritted, acting as a fragile barrier for her rage.

'The old Veronica would never say something like that!'

'Newsflash, Jess: the old Veronica is gone. The sooner you get that into your head, the better.'

The sharp, nasty tone of Veronica's voice stings and Jessica blinks hard, desperately fending off her tears. Before Veronica even has time to think, Jessica lurches forwards, pulling at the designer coat she's wearing, trying to open the pockets.

'Are you using?' Jessica asks, desperation creating ripples in her voice.

'Get off me!' Veronica screams, furiously shoving Jessica away from her. 'This is Karen's jacket, not mine. I'm not going to have anything hidden, am I?'

'Something's not right.'

'You can't search me without good reason.'

'Looks like it's confession time then, doesn't it?'

'I've got nothing to say.'

'Are you an addict?'

'A bit nosey for a minimum-wage-cleaner, aren't you?' Veronica says, glaring at her and Jessica wonders if she's found her out.

'Are you an addict?' Jessica asks again.

Veronica stays silent, but as Jessica watches her squirm she gets the answer she's been dreading. Deep down she knew as soon as she walked back into their lives, but Jessica didn't want to upset her. Scruffy hair, dirty clothes, shaking hands, scratching, mood swings. It's textbook. Suddenly a wave of dread washes over her.

'Are you an alcoholic?' Jessica then asks.

'Too late if I am.' Veronica gestures towards the nearly-empty bottle on the table and Jessica is consumed with guilt.

She should have asked before. 'You're a bit slow, aren't you? Karen guessed straight away.'

'Have you done something bad?'

Again, Veronica falls silent and Jessica finds her answer in her eyes. They dart around the room, looking at everything but her. Textbook.

'What have you done?' Jessica asks, trying her best to stay calm. Her temper is one of her flaws according to her boss.

'Nothing,' she denies, still refusing eye contact.

'Whatever it is, just tell me. I can help you, Veronica,' Jessica tells her, petrified of what she could potentially discover.

Her words seem to fall on deaf ears as Veronica doesn't respond; instead, she chews anxiously on her broken fingernails, flinching as a layer of blood seeps from under her nail, staining her rough skin. Jessica crouches in front of Veronica, lifting her chin so she has no choice but to look her right in the eye, something she can see is hard for her to do.

'See that photo?' Jessica says, turning Veronica's head towards the frame photograph of the five of them.

She sees Veronica's eyes soften a little, making her smile. Jessica wonders if she remembers Tequila Tuesdays.

'Everyone who's ever seen that photo asks if that's my family. You know what I say?' Jessica says, making Veronica look at her. 'Without hesitation, I say yes.'

'It's over now.'

'Feelings never go away, no matter how much time passes. I still love you all.'

'Except Karen?'

'Believe it or not, I never meant to break her heart. I love her like I love you and Bradley and Jason. Friendships like ours don't come along every day. Please let me help?' Jessica pleads, gaining no response. 'If you let me help you then who knows, we could all be happy again, like in that photo.'

'Using our memories to pull at my heartstrings. That's low, Jess, really low.'

'If it makes you open up then I don't care.'

'I have to go.'

'Please don't!' Jessica begs, realising she's pushed her too far.

Veronica quickly gets up from the sofa, making her way to the front door. Jessica rushes after her, clutching her jacket for the second time, this time tighter than before, hungry for more information.

'Jess, I won't tell you again. Get your hands off me!'

She pulls at her coat, making Jessica's hands fall free. Readjusting the baggy clothes she is wearing, a small piece of paper falls from her pocket; but Veronica hasn't realised as she rushes out the front door before the paper hits the ground.

*****

Veronica storms out of the flat, slamming the door as loudly as she possibly can. She's scared. Furious. Embarrassed. She saw the way Jessica looked at her. The way they've all been looking at her. It makes her feel a million times worse, and that's something she thought was impossible.

Jessica's face when she heard her cough . . . anyone would think Veronica had the plague. She's convinced Jessica only offered to take her to the hospital to get her out of her flat. She was probably worried she'd contaminated the room with her germs. Not that Veronica would call that place a palace. With cobwebs inhabiting every corner and a stack

185

of dirty dishes by the sink, it's more like a teenage hideout than a home.

Veronica hears the door slam again, forcing her to turn around and come face to face with Jessica.

'Lost something?' Jessica asks, stony-faced, holding a small piece of paper.

Frantically searching her coat pockets, desperately hoping it isn't true, Veronica's heart plummets when she realises her pockets are completely empty.

'Give it b-back to me,' Veronica stammers.

'"I never meant to hurt you or your family, I'm sorry." Who's this for?' Jessica asks, reciting the words written on the piece of paper.

'No-one.'

'Stop lying to me! You're always lying to me!'

Veronica falls silent, a lump in her throat trapping each breath, not letting them escape. Jessica stays fixated on her the whole time, the enraged glint in her eyes terrifying Veronica.

'It's for Mrs Carter,' Veronica admits, a groan escaping her lips. She'd never said her name out loud before. She doesn't deserve to.

'Mrs Carter?' Jessica asks, so scared her voice is almost a whisper.

'She was married to Mr Carter before . . .' Veronica says before the lump in her throat steals her breath again for a moment. 'Before he was killed.'

'Why do you need to apologise to her?' Jessica asks, although the tears brimming in her eyes tell Veronica she's already worked it out.

'It was me.'

Suddenly Veronica's legs give way and she crumbles to the ground; her knees trembling, her whole body trembling. She feels suffocated, her heart racing with panic as she struggles to catch her breath. Did that just happen? She's been running from that night for longer than she cares to remember . . . and now it's out in the open. A confession in the passageway outside her best friend's flat.

Veronica looks up. Jessica's gone. She wonders if she was ever really there. Was it her mind playing tricks on her? A hallucination? It wouldn't be the first time.

Veronica wants to run, like she did all those years ago. She tries to stand, clinging to the wall, but all feeling has escaped her body. She crashes to the ground once more, the bitter chill of the stone floor biting her cheek.

Jessica emerges from her flat, dragging her feet along the uneven ground until she is standing over Veronica's body. Her pale cheeks are stained with black, mascara-filled tears and her hands are shaking more than Veronica's as she reaches into her back pocket. She pulls out something that, through Veronica's blurred eyes, looks like a small leather wallet. It's only upon closer inspection, when she opens it, that Veronica realises it's her worst nightmare. The thing she's been running from for twenty years.

'DC Jessica Palmer,' she says, holding out the badge, her eyes in the photo glaring at Veronica, burning deep into her skin, paralysing her whole body.

CHAPTER FIFTY-SEVEN
Present Day

Having left their hospital appointment ten minutes ago, Bradley and Danielle are taking some time to get some air and clear their heads. There is often a lot of information at these appointments and it's important they take time out to avoid getting overwhelmed. Although often, it's too late for Danielle. She becomes overwhelmed, in a good way or bad, the moment they step into the doctor's office.

Today, to Bradley's surprise, she's been sitting on this bench in almost complete silence since their appointment has ended. Bradley wants to support her as best as he can, but he has to choose his words carefully.

'I know the appointment didn't exactly go to plan today . . .' Bradley says, preparing himself for one of Danielle's mood swings.

'What are you talking about? It was great,' Danielle replies.

'You think so?' Bradley asks.

'The doctor said I'm okay to go for another round,' Danielle says, a grin appearing on her face, just at the mention of it.

'Yeah, if we can afford it, which we can't right now,' Bradley says.

'Why are you trying to bring me down?' Danielle asks, feeling disheartened, and as much as Bradley feels guilty, he always knows he's talking sense. It isn't the right time.

'I'm not. I'd never do that,' Bradley says, taking her hands in his. 'What brings you down is negative pregnancy test after negative pregnancy test.'

'It will be positive one day,' Danielle says.

'Of course it will. We'll get there eventually, but for now, let's take a breather. Give your body time to recover after the last round,' Bradley replies.

'You promise we won't give up?' Danielle says, looking at her husband expectantly, like a needy child. Normally it irritates him, but today Bradley has more patience with her. It's always the way after an IVF consultation.

'I promise,' Bradley reassures her, placing a loving kiss on the top of her head.

CHAPTER FIFTY-EIGHT
Present Day

Karen's pacing the floor, anxiously biting at her manicured nails – only for a brief moment, though, and then she stops herself. It wouldn't look good for business, a beautician with chewed nails. They've been back at her apartment for an hour and she's yet to sit and relax. She refused a coffee and has been barely speaking to Jason, instead checking her phone and watch every thirty seconds. Jason noticed she took her heels off immediately, her bare feet in direct contact with the cold floor.

Jason hates to see her so stressed and he wishes he could take it away. He gets up from his seat and goes over to her, wrapping his arm round her shoulders, stopping her in her tracks. She relaxes in his embrace for a moment before she shrugs him off and begins pacing again.

'What's up?' Jason asks.

'I thought Veronica would be back right now,' Karen says, checking her watch again.

'Maybe she's enjoying herself at Jessica's place. They haven't really had a proper catch up, just the two of them,' Jason says, wanting to offer her some reassurance. Truth is, he's worried too. Veronica didn't seem in a good way that morning, but he didn't want to do anything to upset Karen further.

'I'll give Jess a call,' she tells him.

'Don't get yourself so worked up,' Jason replies, keen to look after her. 'We didn't give Jess a specific time to have her home.'

'They were supposed to be back at five. What if she's done a runner? She won't last much longer on the streets,' she says, her voice quivering with worry.

'Given the choice, anyone would live here rather than on the streets.'

'Well, obviously she wouldn't choose a life on the streets, Jason, but she's an addict. What if she's gone in search of a fix? It's so dangerous out there.'

'She'll be fine. Jess will be looking after her,' Jason says, trying to take her mobile from her hands. He doesn't want her putting herself under too much stress.

'Even so, I'm going to call her,' she says, moving so Jason can't reach her anymore.

Karen calls Jessica's number, pressing the phone to her ear. She immediately starts tapping her foot, anxious as she waits for a response.

'No answer,' she says, ending the call and throwing her phone into her handbag. 'I'm going round there.'

'Are you sure you're not over-reacting?'

'I told her I'd look after her, and I'm worried, so no, it's not an over-reaction. You're going to have to go home. Better not stay here alone,' Karen tells him and he can see her eyes scan the room, probably checking that they're not leaving it in a lived-in state. It must be sterile, free from people, free from feeling. Just like her husband.

'I'm coming with you,' Jason says, grabbing his coat from the arm of the sofa to ease her worries.

'You don't have to,' she says, shaking her head.

'You promised Veronica you'd look after her, and I promised I'd look after you. Neither of us are letting anyone down,' Jason tells her.

'Thank you,' she says, offering me a kind smile.

Jason takes her hand, wanting to stop it shaking. He doesn't know whether it's shaking through fear or through worry, or perhaps even through excitement that he's here with her again; but whatever it is, Jason wants to make it stop. He expects her to pull away immediately, the way she has done every day since the reunion party, but she doesn't. For a moment, just for a moment, she allows their hands to connect, their fingers to intertwine with one another, their skin to touch.

Then she does it, the thing Jason's been waiting for.

She pulls away.

*****

Banging her fist against Jessica's front door, her heart racing, Jason tries to pull Karen away. Normally Karen would do as he says but consumed with worry for Veronica, she keeps hammering the door until Jessica opens it.

'What's the point of having a phone if you're not gonna answer it?' Karen says, knocking into her as she barges into the flat.

'Hello to you too,' Jessica mutters sarcastically.

Jason follows Karen into the flat and Jessica closes the front door, leaning against it, as if wanting to keep her distance from them. Jason stands beside Karen, resting his hand on the small of her back and he smiles at Bradley, who's sitting on the sofa, looking a little uncomfortable.

'Save the false pleasantries. I've come to collect Veronica,' Karen tells her, already sick of hearing her voice.

'She's not here.'

'What?'

'You heard.'

'Where is she?' Karen asks, and for the first time since arriving, Karen notices how awful Jessica looks. Her skin is pale and clammy and her eyes red-raw as if she's been crying. It panics her.

Karen waits for a response but Jessica keeps quiet, so free of any sort of emotion that she looks like a robot guarding the front door. After staring at her for a few moments, Jessica shrugs her shoulders.

'Jess! She must have said something,' Karen says, angered by her casual attitude. It's like getting blood out of a stone.

'She just went off when my back was turned,' she tells Karen.

'Why did you give her the chance to run off?' Karen asks. She'd made such good progress with Veronica and, in a matter of hours, Jess has undone it all.

Yet again Jessica ignores her, choosing to pick the coffee mugs up from the table, obviously wanting an excuse to leave the room. Karen snatches them from her hands so fast that a couple of splashes of leftover coffee land on her blouse. Her white blouse. That'll stain. Paul will be furious, especially given the price tag, but right now, Karen couldn't care less. Veronica is more important.

'Jess, she's a vulnerable woman. We're supposed to be looking after her,' Karen says.

'She's better off on the streets,' Jess replies.

'When did you become so heartless?'

'How are we supposed to do anything when we don't know where she's gone? Just forget about her.'

'*Forget about her*? She's our friend. Forgetting her isn't an option,' Karen says, stunned. How can she be so calm about this, so casual? They used to be so close that people mistook them for being family. They used to care about one another.

'Is that what we are now? Only it seemed some of us were more of an embarrassment to you,' Jessica says.

'Enough! This isn't about us, it's about Veronica. I agree with Karen, I think she could be in serious trouble,' Jason says, finally growing some backbone and standing up to Jessica, instead of constantly trying to make her feel comfortable.

'Did you two have a row?' Karen asks Jessica.

'Could say that,' Jess says, although she avoids making eye contact with them. She's obviously guilty.

'Oh, well, there we go then, you scared her off this time. God knows what state her head's in now,' Karen says, completely despairing over her former best friend's attitude.

'So what are you gonna do? Search the city again until you find her?' Jess asks, glaring at her as if she's stupid.

'If that's what it takes.'

'And then you'll take her in again, yeah? Because you did a brilliant job last time,' Jess says, mocking Karen. She makes her blood boil, she really does.

'At least I made the effort.'

'What do you expect me to do? It's not like I can have her stay with me.'

'Why not? You've got a sofa she can sleep on and food in the fridge. That's all she needs.'

'I haven't got the room,' Jessica says, the coldness in her tone of voice shocking Karen. They used to be willing to do anything for each other.

'You *make* room!' Karen shouts, desperate to get through to Jessica, completely disgusted by her lack of empathy for Veronica.

'You're the rich one,' she says, jealousy lacing her words.

'And she was perfectly happy in my spare room until you started picking on her,' Karen says.

'Who the hell do you think you are, eh? Stood there in your designer clothes and heels, not a hair out of place. You've been looking down your nose at me since the party and I'm sick of it,' Jessica replies, practically snarling at Karen.

'Sounds a lot like jealousy to me.'

'Did you not hear me before? This isn't about your stupid little feud!' Jason snaps, glaring angrily at both Karen and Jessica.

'*Stupid little feud*?' Karen asks, stunned that he could even refer to it as that. It's not stupid. It never has been. It was real and it broke her heart.

'This is about Veronica. We need to put any other feelings aside and focus on her,' Jason says.

'I agree,' Bradley says, finally joining the conversation. He'd been so distant.

'We need to find her as soon as possible. If she's angry and upset, anything could happen to her. The streets are dangerous, especially for an addict,' Karen says again, desperately.

'I've got work in a few hours so I won't be joining the search party,' Jessica says casually.

'Take the day off. We'd all do the same.'

'I can't afford to pull a sickie.'

'Saving a friend's life is hardly pulling a sickie.'

'A bit dramatic don't you think?' Jess rolls her eyes.

'Jess, you're coming with us,' Jason tells her, firmly.

'Do you want to see me out on the streets too? What kind of life will Natalie have? She's fourteen years old. She wouldn't survive living rough,' Jess says.

'Now who's being dramatic?' Karen replies, sharply, angered by the mention of their teenage daughter.

'I'll pay you double what you would have earned tonight,' Jason offers.

Karen clenches her fists once again. He's playing right into Jessica's hands.

'I don't know . . .' Jessica sighs.

'Four pairs of eyes are better than three,' Jason replies.

'Please Jess? She's ill and she's an addict. We need to find her. It's important,' Bradley tells her.

'Not to me it isn't,' Jessica says.

'Do you know what, just leave her. She's shown where her loyalties lie,' Karen replies, glaring at her. 'Have a nice life, Jess.'

Karen slams the door as she and Jason leave, immediately filling the room with silence.

Bradley watches Jessica for a while. He watches her pace the room. He watches as she slowly clenches her fists, as Karen had done, as if suppressing anger . . . although for once, Bradley doesn't think her anger is directed at Karen.

'Why do I get the impression there's more to this than a row?' Bradley asks.

CHAPTER FIFTY-NINE
Present Day

The night of the reunion, one hundred and four people walked in and out of the door. Today, just ten. Everything looks different during the day. Less glamorous, less lively. Veronica's not entirely sure why she came here. Running from Jessica's place, she seemed to let her legs decide her destination. Although, as her legs became weaker and weaker she feared she'd end up in a heap in the middle of the road. Perhaps that would have been the best thing for everyone.

She wishes she'd never sat on this bench a couple of nights ago. She's spent the last twenty years dreaming of the moment they'd all reunite, hoping they'd get that spark back, but now that they have come back together, she'd do anything to erase it. It's not that she regrets meeting them, or that she doesn't care. She just doesn't deserve their love.

A siren blares in her ears, making her jump so much she's sure her heart actually stops beating for a while. She has no idea where it's coming from and it scares her. She wants to run but a painful ache sears through her legs and she knows she won't get far. She also wants to look around, search for the cop car, but her eyes seem paralysed, focusing on the social club. It could be fear or it could be her hangover. Either way, Veronica can't seem to move.

Then the siren fades into the distance and she knows she's safe, for now at least. She's sure it won't be long before the police come calling, probably with Jessica leading the investigation. Veronica sighs loudly and her heart begins beating again, once again a little faster than normal.

*****

She looks so small sat on the bench all on her own. Like a lost kid or, with her make-up wiped away, revealing her pale complexion and the hangover that's obviously starting to kick in, a ghost. It's a warm day but she pulls her knees up to her chest, hugging them tightly, as if it's a freezing winter morning. She looks so lost.

Karen starts walking towards the bench and Jason follows, keeping as close to her as he possibly can.

'Leave it to me,' Karen tells him, placing a hand on his chest to prevent him going any further.

'I'm not gonna upset her,' he says.

'I know, but we've been getting on really well. We've made a connection. Just let me do this,' Karen replies.

Jason hesitates for a moment before nodding his head, agreeing with her. Karen smiles gratefully, glad of his support, and slowly makes her way to Veronica. She doesn't want to startle her, but there's no disguising the sound of her heels, and her friend's head snaps round. It's immediately clear she's annoyed that they've tracked her down.

'Why do you keep following me?' Veronica asks.

'If you don't want to be found then I reckon you need to find some better hiding places,' Karen says, trying to lighten the mood. Veronica used to be well-known for her smile. It could light up a room. Now, the smiles come in short supply. Karen doesn't blame her though.

'I mean it, Karen, why are you here?' Veronica asks, more firmly than before.

'Because I'm worried about you,' Karen tells her.

'There's no need.' She shakes her head, refusing to look at her.

'Jess said you did a runner,' Karen replies.

'What else did she say?' Veronica asks, suddenly looking at Karen, her eyes wide and bulging in her face.

'Nothing. She's in a right mood back at hers. It's doing my head in.'

'Is she looking for me too?'

'I don't know.'

'I've got to go,' Veronica says, getting up from the bench, letting out an exhausted groan as she does so. Karen tries to reach for her but Veronica dodges her hand.

'Where?' Karen asks.

'Anywhere. I just can't stay here,' Veronica says, out of breath, full of panic.

'Veronica, what's going on?'

'Nothing.'

'What happened between you and Jess?' Karen asks, and she realises her tone of voice is quite harsh. She's not angry with Veronica. It's Jess who's wound her up. It's obvious there's more to Veronica being on the streets than she's told them, but instead of finding out, Jess has kicked her to the curb. She's so selfish.

Veronica doesn't speak, only pauses for a split second before starting to walk away. But not towards Jason, in the opposite direction. Away from both of them.

'Please don't run away,' Karen calls after her.

Veronica's not listening to her, Karen can tell. She's got no intention of stopping, so Karen goes after her, desperate to help. She won't be able to live with herself if she lets her walk away. She's so weak and vulnerable, she won't last the year. As

Karen get closer to her, Veronica tries and fails to pick up her speed, limping and shuffling like an elderly woman, letting out the occasional whimper of pain.

'You've been running for the last twenty years. Please just stop,' Karen pleads, stopping Veronica in her tracks, pulling her round.

'I can't,' she says, trying to wrestle herself from Karen's grip, but years on the streets are seriously taking their toll on her health. She has no strength.

'Come back to mine. You can still have the spare room.'

'What about your husband?'

'He's not around, you know that.'

'What if he comes back?'

'I'll deal with him.'

'He won't want me there, making the place look untidy,' Veronica says, wearily shaking her head.

'At least it'll look lived in, instead of a show home,' Karen says, smiling at Veronica, who doesn't return the gesture.

'I can't,' Veronica replies.

'You spend any more time on the streets and you'll end up seriously ill, or worse,' Karen says as tears fill her eyes. She can't bear the thought of losing Veronica. They've been apart for so long but she always clung on to the fact that they'd meet again. If she doesn't take care of herself, they'll never see each other. There'll be no more reunions, no more friendship. All those years would go, just like that.

'I'm not your problem,' Veronica says.

'I'm making you my problem,' Karen says, her eyes locked with Veronica's. 'Come on, what's all this about?'

'It was me. I did it,' Veronica says quickly, letting out a

massive sigh, as if all her troubles have escaped. Like she's been holding onto something.

'Did what?'

Karen waits, looking into Veronica's eyes, watching them dart around the street, focusing on everything but her. Then Veronica's hand falls on her scrawny wrist; the daisy chain tattoo identical to Karen's. She knows Veronica's trying to distract her. She wants a quick getaway.

'Veronica! Did what?' Karen asks, perhaps raising her voice a little too loud but she needs to know.

'I killed Mr Carter.'

*****

Veronica's eyes are clamped shut and she can't hear anything. Not a sound. Karen's probably done a runner, wanting to get away from her as soon as possible. All the help and support she's offered her these past few days, all gone. Wasted on a monster like her.

Eventually, Veronica plucks up the courage to open one eye, expecting to find herself standing alone in the street; instead, she finds Karen standing in the same spot, holding out her hand, a gentle expression on her face. Veronica opens her other eye, just to check she is actually seeing things correctly.

She is. Karen's still willing to support her, despite what she's just told her. Maybe she didn't hear her right.

'What?' Veronica asks, having expected a verbal beating, not the kind offering of Karen's hand.

'You're coming back with me.'

'I already said no.'

'I'm not taking no for an answer. Come on, we'll look after you,' Karen says, trying to take her hand again, but Veronica snatches it away.

'We?' Veronica asks. There hasn't been a "we" in so long that it still takes her by surprise when Karen says it.

'Me and Jason and Bradley and Jess.'

'No.'

'They're your friends and they love you.'

'Not anymore,' Veronica says, her voice quiet. If she speaks any louder then it might actually register with her body; and if she starts crying, she knows she won't stop.

'Does Jess know about this?' Karen asks.

'I'd written a note . . . to Mrs Carter. It didn't say a lot, but I just felt I needed to do it,' Veronica replies.

'What did it say?' Karen asks.

Veronica wishes she'd stop asking questions. She doesn't want to relive the moment anymore.

'That I'm sorry. I am sorry, Karen. I'm so sorry for what I did,' Veronica says, tears brimming in her eyes. She bites her lip hard to stop it quivering.

'I know.'

'Me and Jess had a row and it fell out of my pocket.'

Karen doesn't say anything, still taking everything in. Veronica hopes she doesn't hate her. She couldn't stand it if she lost her too. Karen and Jason are the only ones who actually want to bother with her; the only people who have given her a second glance, and haven't judged her.

Veronica finds herself falling against Karen, letting her wrap her arms around her. She hasn't been hugged by anyone for a long time. She's forgotten how comforting it feels. She wishes they could stay like this forever. It feels like nothing and no-one can get to her. It feels like she's safe, like she can't be taken away.

But at the same time, she's so frightened.

'She's gonna send me to prison,' Veronica tells Karen.

'Friends don't do that to each other.'

'No, but coppers do.'

'Copper?' Karen says, stunned.

'Jessica's a police officer,' Veronica replies, pulling away from Karen, her voice trembling as the memories of a few hours earlier flash in front of her eyes.

'You must have got confused. She's a cleaner in a hotel,' Karen says.

'Then why did she show me her police badge? I told her the truth, and she disappeared into her flat and came back out a few seconds later carrying her police badge.'

'Looks like it's mine and Jason's job to look after you then,' Karen replies, once again holding out her hand, only this time, Veronica takes it.

CHAPTER SIXTY
Present Day

Bradley is sitting beside Jessica in the exact places they've been in for the past couple of hours. They'd passed the time with small talk. It wasn't really what Bradley wanted to do. He wanted to find out what had gone on with Jessica and Veronica, but Jessica hadn't been in the mood to indulge him in the details. The room fell silent and Bradley couldn't hold himself back any longer. He'd spent the afternoon away from Danielle when she really needed him, so the least he deserved was the truth.

'So what happened?' Bradley asks, immediately capturing Jessica's attention.

'When?' Jessica replies, innocently, although it doesn't wash with Bradley. She's hiding something. It's obvious.

'When Veronica was here,' Bradley says.

'I've already said. She didn't fancy sticking round,' Jessica says.

'But why?' Bradley asks, glaring at his friend. Something's not right about this.

'I don't know.'

'Jess . . .'

'What? She's obviously got a screw loose if she keeps doing a runner every opportunity she gets.'

'You used to be so close,' Bradley says. It's been difficult for him to comprehend the change in his friends, the state of their once-unbreakable bond.

'We were all close to her,' Jessica says.

'And we all want to help her,' Bradley replies.

'Veronica used to say she loved us but it must have been a lie, otherwise why would she have upped and left like she did?' Jessica says, once again trying to avoid the subject.

'That was twenty years ago. You can't still be holding a grudge?' Bradley tells her. Five little kids who loved each other more than anything, to five adults who can barely be in the same room as each other. He can barely believe it's come to this. He doesn't want to believe it.

'I wasn't, no, but it looks like history has repeated itself. There are only so many chances you can give someone.'

CHAPTER SIXTY-ONE
Present Day

Veronica is huddled in the back seat of Karen's car. She should feel comfortable, enveloped in the plush leather seats but she doesn't. She won't ever feel comfortable again. Everything's changed and she's is feeling more suffocated by the second.

'Please stop the car,' Veronica begs, her heart practically in her mouth, beating so hard she swears it'll burst out of her body any second.

'Why?' Karen asks. She doesn't slow down at all.

'You shouldn't have to do this,' Veronica tells her.

'It's what friends are for,' Karen replies, so casually that Veronica, and even Jason, can barely believe her attitude. It's as if she hasn't fully taken in what Veronica has confessed, like it will hit her later, suddenly.

'You don't need people like me in your life. You've got enough trouble with your husband.'

'This is completely different. You deserve my time. My waste-of-space husband doesn't.'

'I'm don't think many people would agree with you,' Veronica says. Her eyes flick to Jason, who has remained frozen, silent, in the passenger seat. Karen doesn't notice though.

'I don't care,' Karen says.

'Doesn't it bother you? What I did?' Veronica asks.

She'd expected them to react the same way as Jessica, or worse: shout, scream, hit her, shop her to the police. It would be a thing of nightmares if Jason and Karen were also police officers. Actually, this *is* the thing of nightmares. This. Right here. Waiting for a response from her friends, wondering if they're about to change their minds and kick her to the curb. Veronica wouldn't blame them.

'You were pushed to it. It doesn't make it right. Nothing can ever make it right. But you've punished yourself more than enough. Right now you need our help,' Karen says, finally turning her attention to a shell-shocked Jason. 'I'm right aren't I, Jase?'

Jason remains silent.

CHAPTER SIXTY-TWO
Present Day

Bradley watches as Jessica starts pacing the room again. He knows he's driving her mad with his constant questions but he's not giving up. There's something going on. Something huge. Something life-changing. If there wasn't, then why isn't Jessica just coming clean. Why the secrets?

'I'm not going until you tell me,' Bradley tells her.

'You can stay as long as you like but we're changing the subject,' Jessica replies.

'Veronica must have really upset you.'

'I'm fine.'

'You don't look fine,' Bradley says, studying her face: dark circles, pale complexion. She looks like she's going to keel over at any moment.

'It's been a weird couple of days. Haven't slept much,' Jessica says.

'I doubt you'll sleep tonight either, given what you know about Veronica,' Bradley says, not taking my eyes off her.

'What?' Jessica replies.

'You must know something and I'm guessing it's something pretty bad. You'd never have let her run off–'

'What part of *I don't want to talk about it* don't you understand?' Jessica snaps, shutting Bradley down.

The room is once again silent and Bradley casually scans the room, the layout of the flat, as much as he can with Jessica still pacing.

'I'm just gonna nip to the loo. Is that okay?' Bradley asks, a little sheepishly, given Jessica's outburst.

'Sure.'

Bradley gets up from the sofa, initially looking like he is heading for the bathroom, when Jessica suddenly realises he is about to open her bedroom door instead.

'What are you doing? The bathroom's . . .'

Bradley doesn't pay any attention to what Jessica is saying and grabs the door handle, revealing Jessica's bedroom. It doesn't take him long to realise why Jessica has been so cagey: there's a police uniform hanging neatly on the wardrobe door.

'So, this is the big secret?' Bradley says, turning to look at Jessica, making her heart sink. She's been rumbled.

CHAPTER SIXTY-THREE
Present Day

Karen comes through, having settled Veronica back in the spare room. Jason gets up from the sofa and turns to face his ex-girlfriend. It's a relief, to be honest: he couldn't sit still, couldn't relax. Perhaps it's got something to do with Karen's decision. He can't believe it. She thinks everything will turn out fine. That if they put Veronica in the spare room, hide her away, then they'll be able to get on with their lives.

But this is huge. Jason knew something was going on with Veronica but he never, in a million years, thought it would be something like this. She took a man's life. A man they knew. A man that taught them.

How could she? Why would she? And more than that: how can Karen even contemplate taking Veronica's side?

*****

He's looking at Karen like she's a stranger. It hurts her to see him like that. He said he'd support her and now that things are getting tough, it seems he wants out. Typical Jason. He's probably looking for an escape route so he can shack up with Jess and play happy families with her and Natalie.

'You can't do this.'

'Why not? It's my home. Or at least it's supposed to be.'

'She could be dangerous.'

'She's so weak she can barely lift her hands above her head. She couldn't be any less dangerous if she tried.'

'I don't want you getting hurt,' Jason tells her, and Karen has to admit she gets a kick out of him trying to protect her. The moments where he's focused on her and no-one else. It's a refreshing change to have someone care for her but, right now, her only priority is keeping Veronica safe. No matter what the price.

'So let me do this. She's my friend, our friend, and she made a terrible mistake . . . but don't you think she's paid the price?' Karen says.

'Okay, so you'll let Veronica sleep in the spare room. What happens when Paul comes home?' he asks. 'Do you really think you can just barricade the door and stop him from ever going in there? Stop Veronica ever coming out?'

'I think it's highly unlikely he'll come home anytime soon, don't you?' Karen says.

'He could walk through that door at any minute,' Jason says – although Karen thinks he's more worried about the two of them being found together by her husband than by Veronica being here.

'I'll just say she's an old school friend. I won't be lying, will I?' Karen says.

'What about when Amelia comes home for the holidays and she's got nowhere to sleep? How are you gonna explain why she's been relegated to the sofa?' Jason asks.

'We'll sort something. Maybe it's time for a bigger place anyway,' Karen says, glancing round the apartment. She'd love nothing more than to leave this place.

'You're being ridiculous.'

'Why don't you say what you really think, eh? Go on, don't hold back.'

'I just can't believe you'd be willing to have Amelia live under the same roof as a killer.'

211

'She wouldn't hurt her. Veronica's a mother herself,' Karen says.

'A mother that hasn't seen her kid for God knows how long,' Jason replies.

His words are harsh and Karen can understand his reasoning, but she just can't turn her back on Veronica. It's too much.

*****

Veronica has her ear pressed up against the door, hearing every word of her friends' conversation. The mention of her son strikes a chord, and a sharp pain through her heart. She misses him every day, despite never really having had the chance to get to know him. She opens the bedroom door, making Karen and Jason pause their conversation and turn their attention to her.

'I'm gonna go,' Veronica says. She won't come between Karen and Jason. They don't deserve it.

'No, you're not,' Karen tells her, standing in front of the door, using her whole body as a barrier, sort of like a shield, keeping her safe from the outside world.

'Jason's right. You shouldn't be doing this for me,' Veronica says.

'Stay in the spare room. We're going to Jessica's,' Karen replies.

'Why?' Veronica asks, the mention of her former friend making her heart pound with panic.

'Don't worry, we'll talk to her, make her see sense,' Karen says, trying to offer Veronica some reassurance.

It's not working.

'You really think you can talk her round? You think all you have to do is say please and she'll let me off the hook?'

'It's worth a try.'

'Except you two hate each other's guts. Why would she want to do anything to help you?'

'Because she owes me. Big time,' Karen says, her eyes flicking to Jason for a brief moment.

As Veronica watches her take the apartment keys from her bag, gripping them tightly in her hand, she panics. She doesn't want her to go. Or Jason. She can't be on her own. She's so tired of being on her own.

'What are you doing?' Veronica asks.

'I'm gonna lock you in, okay? It's the safest thing,' Karen tells Veronica as she opens the front door. 'And I want you to put the chain across once we're gone. Everything's going to be fine.'

'Until Paul comes home and tries to let himself in. He's gonna get the shock of his life,' Jason says.

'He's not coming home today,' Karen says.

'You *think* he's not coming home today,' Jason replies. Veronica can tell he is deeply worried for Karen.

'I know. He called me earlier today, at the usual time, saying he had another very important meeting and that he won't be home until tomorrow,' Karen says before she and Jason leave the apartment.

Veronica hears the rattling of the key in the other side of the door and she does as Karen says, putting the chain on, adding a bit of extra security. Not that she feels particularly secure. Every noise, every flash of light, makes her jump out of her skin.

Then there's silence.

CHAPTER SIXTY-FOUR
Present Day

As they make their way towards Jessica's flat, the front door opens and they're face to face with Natalie. She looks good, like she did yesterday, in a pair of skinny jeans and a little crop top that shows off her flat stomach. Karen remembers being her age and trying to experiment with different fashions. When she looks at photographs, she realises she didn't pull it off very well, although Jessica and Veronica were in the same boat. But Natalie looks cool and stylish, like she's got everything under control. Just like her father.

Natalie offers Karen a kind smile, but she doesn't return the gesture. It's too soon. She can't. Not yet. For a brief moment Natalie looks at Jason and he looks at her.

'Hi,' Natalie says.

'Hi. How are you?' Jason asks.

'Good thanks, are you?' she replies.

'Yeah,' he nods, seeming a little nervous, although he doesn't take his eyes off her.

'I'm just heading into town, meeting some friends,' Natalie tells him. It makes Karen angry.

'At this time?' he asks.

'Mum said it's fine,' she replies, sounding like the perfect little daughter, asking Mum and Dad's permission.

'Fair enough. Keep safe, though, won't you?' he tells her.

'I will. Bye,' she replies.

Jason smiles as he watches Natalie walk away. It's not a

normal smile either. It's a proud smile. He's proud of her. His daughter with Jessica.

'Fitting right into the protective father role,' Karen mutters, her blood boiling.

*****

Karen bangs her fist against the front door, and as soon Jessica's opens it she barges past her. Jason follows, as fast as he can, giving Jessica a gentle smile as he walks into the flat. She seems a little shaken, almost as if she's been crying, and she wearily closes the door.

Bradley's sitting on the sofa, finishing a mug of coffee, looking almost as traumatised as Jessica. It doesn't take a genius to work out what he and Jess had been discussing before they arrived. Bradley was always the strong one at school, never crying, never complaining. It wasn't that he was cold or lacking in feelings, it was just that he'd take it upon himself to be their tower of strength, making sure he was there for whichever one of them needed advice or a helping hand. It's hard to see him so down.

'I gather she's filled you in on the details,' Karen says, looking at Bradley, her arms folded, as if conducting an important business meeting. No emotion. No feeling.

'About Veronica? Yeah,' Bradley says.

'How do you know?' Jessica asks, stunned.

'She just confessed everything to me,' Karen tells her.

'Where's Veronica now?' Bradley asks.

'You let her run off I hope,' Jessica says, keeping her eyes fixed on Karen.

'Course I didn't. She's safe,' Karen says, as if she thinks she needs reassuring.

'I couldn't care less how she is. I want her to stay away from me,' Jessica replies.

'Bradley . . .' Karen says, turning her attention to her calmer, more mature friend.

'If she comes anywhere near me, I'm not sure I'll be able to control my actions, and I really, really don't want to be anything like her,' Bradley warns Karen. This shocks them all. He's never been like that in his life. He's not got a violent or angry bone in his body.

'She's got a name,' Karen snaps.

'She's not worthy of one,' Bradleys says sharply.

'Are you seriously going to turn your back on her?' Karen asks, completely broken-hearted by the turn of events. How did it come to this?

'There's no other option,' Bradley tells her, a rage building inside his body.

'Walking away is the only one,' Jessica says.

'Here we go, offering words of wisdom, *DC Palmer*,' Karen says, letting out a small laugh, although there isn't anything about this situation remotely humorous.

'And I'll be using my position within the force to make sure Veronica pays for what she's done,' Jessica tells them, coldly.

'You bitch!' Karen snarls through gritted teeth.

Before anyone has a chance to digest what's going on, Karen launches herself at Jessica, like a wild beast that's been freed from a cage, grabbing her hair, digging her manicured nails right into Jessica's scalp. Karen pulls at her like a rag doll, and pain sears from Jessica's head all the way down her body, her cheeks burning with humiliation. Her heart's racing, her hands shaking. She tries to shove her off but she can't: she's almost paralysed with shock.

'Stop it, Karen! Get off her. Let go!' Jason shouts, dragging Karen away from Jessica.

'There's only one way this can end, Karen. You know it as well as we do,' Bradley says.

'I know you care about her deep down. If you didn't, you would have handed her in by now,' Karen says, pure desperation in her voice, staring at Jessica as if trying to convince her to change her mind.

'I'm biding my time. Keeping her on her toes. She's put the Carter family through absolute hell, so let's see how she likes it,' Jessica says, composing herself. Deep down, she takes no pleasure in this at all. She wishes things were different but they're not. Their friendship means nothing anymore, especially after Karen's outburst.

'That's cruel. You can't do that to her. She's a human being,' Karen says, before turning to Bradley. 'And I know you love her. You love us all. That's why you tracked us down.'

'It's different now,' Bradley says.

'It doesn't have to be,' Karen says, literally begging her friends. 'Jess, please don't hand her in. No-one will ever know. Your boss will never find out, I promise.'

'I haven't told you the reason my marriage is so strained, have I?' Bradley suddenly says.

'No.' Karen shakes her head.

'Danielle, my wife, she lost her father many years ago. She's never got over it,' he tells them.

'I'm sorry to hear that,' Karen says, bowing her head. She knows how it feels to lose a parent.

'It's hard to get over the fact your father was murdered and his killer was never found,' Bradley says.

'Murdered?' Karen says.

'My wife's name is Danielle Knight, but before we married, she was called Danielle *Carter* . . .' Bradley replies.

Watching as Karen's expression changes from desperation to one of pure shock, Jessica, Bradley and Jason realise that this really is the end, that nothing will ever be the same again. A deafening silence fills the room as Karen's eyes drop to the floor. She had to admit to feeling slightly guilty for siding with Veronica, defending her, making her out to be a good person when she's pretty much broken the Carter family; but Veronica has told her about what Brian did, and she's still committed to protecting her.

'Finally put two and two together, have you? Veronica didn't just kill a teacher, she killed my wife's father,' Bradley says, letting all his anger boil to the surface.

'It was self-defence!' Karen says. 'He tried to attack her.'

'We've only got her word for that and, right now, that doesn't count for much,' Bradley mutters.

'She's never been a liar,' Karen says.

'She killed someone and then went on the run. That's the biggest lie there is,' Jessica replies.

'The only liar round here that I can see is you,' Karen says, shooting Jessica a nasty glare.

'No matter what you think, she's going to prison.'

'You can't hand her in.'

'It's my job.'

'You're not even working on this case,' Karen says. 'The case is closed.'

'And?' Jessica asks, shrugging her shoulders. 'I'll get it reopened.'

'Go to the police and Veronica's finished,' Karen says, as if Jessica doesn't already know.

'If I don't hand her in and they find out I knew all along I'll lose my job. Do you have any idea how hard I've worked to get to this point? I won't have her ruin it,' Jessica replies.

'What happened to our friendship?' Karen asks.

'The only way my daughter – sorry, *our* daughter – has been supported over the last fourteen years is by *my* income. We lose that and we'll be homeless. Do you really want to see your daughter out on the street?' Jessica asks, turning her attention to Jason.

'I'll help you,' Jason says.

'How? If we don't go to the police with the information we've got, then we'll all suffer. I'll be homeless and you'll be facing prison.'

'Why? We've done nothing but care for our friend, which is more than can be said for you,' Karen says, defending her actions.

'Yeah, you cared so much you've been letting her stay with you and offered her a job in your salon. You're harbouring a criminal, Karen. That's a criminal offence,' Jessica replies, before once again looking at Jason. 'How do you think that would make Natalie feel? She's on the streets with her mother and her father's in prison.'

'Stop bringing her into this,' Karen says, huffing like a small child having a tantrum.

'Jealousy really is a disgusting trait to have,' Jessica says, remaining calm and collected. She'd normally fly off the handle at this point but she's realised it winds Karen up more if she remains emotionless.

'You're using that kid to pull at his heartstrings. We want to help Veronica because that's what friends do.'

'Our friendship ended twenty years ago.'

'Not for some of us,' she says, glancing at Jessica and then Jason and back again.

'I knew you were jealous. I told you, didn't I?' Jessica says, feeling a smirk creep onto her lips.

'You two are the reason I left uni in the first place, so excuse me if I'm getting tired of hearing about your precious Natalie,' Karen replies, getting worked up. She knew this was coming. When it comes to her and Jason, she can never keep her cool. Jessica watches, still smirking, as Karen clenches her fists even more tightly than before.

'Alright, let's just chill out, shall we?' Jason says, placing a hand on Karen's arm, as if expecting her to launch herself at Jessica again at any moment.

'*Chill out*? She's threatening to send Veronica to prison,' Karen tells him, as if he's been absent from the room. When Jason doesn't respond, Karen snatches her arm away from Jason's grip.

'She deserves it,' Jessica says.

'When did you become Mr Carter's biggest fan?' Karen asks.

'It's my job,' Jessica reminds Karen, feeling smug. For the first time in her life, Jessica has all the power. She is in complete control instead of hiding in the other girls' shadows.

'So you keep saying, but even coppers have hearts. What about all the happy memories we've got from when we were kids? All those nights out where we'd laugh so much we could barely catch our breath? That kind of love can't be recreated. Surely that's got to count for something?' Karen says, softening towards Jessica.

It won't work. Their friendship is over.

'I've got new friends now.'

'Have you? Because I don't see people queuing up at your front door and your phone hasn't gone off once.'

'And you're Little Miss Popular, are you?'

'No actually. I haven't got any friends. Don't let the designer clothes and the posh apartment fool you. I'm just as lonely as you.'

'Clinging on to Veronica won't do you any good. She's bad news, Karen, and we're better off without her.'

'Veronica can't go to prison.'

'Thank God you're not a judge or there would be a lot of empty cells,' Jessica says.

'She won't survive a week inside, let alone a life sentence,' Karen says, her voice more desperate than Jessica's ever heard it before.

'I don't care,' Bradley says, although he doesn't look at Karen, keeping his head lowered.

'Bradley . . .' Karen sighs.

'Don't tell me I'm being harsh, Karen. She did a terrible thing and she deserves everything she gets,' Bradley tells her.

'I wonder if you'd still be saying that if you weren't married to Danielle?' Karen says.

'You haven't seen her like I have. The state she's in on the anniversary of his death, on his birthday, on Father's Day. She was deprived of a relationship with her dad because of what Veronica did,' Bradley explains.

'And I feel for her, of course I do,' Karen says.

'I thought you'd be a little more understanding. After all, you know what it's like to lose a parent,' Bradley says.

'Don't compare my father to hers. My dad was a good man,' Karen says, warning Bradley. She's never lost her temper with Bradley before. They used to be thick as thieves. They all did.

'And so was Brian,' Bradley says.

'Until he tried it on with Veronica,' Karen reminds him. 'His student.'

'Oh please, are you really saying you believe her?' Bradley asks, shaking his head in disbelief.

'Why else would she do a thing like that?' Karen asks.

Karen looks at each of them, as if waiting for them to come around to her way of thinking, but the room remains silent.

'Her life has been hard enough without being sent down. She's punished herself more than any court ever could,' Karen says.

'As much as it pains me to say it, she needs to be put behind bars. If it was anyone else . . .' Jason says, placing his hand on Karen's back, rubbing it gently. He could always sense when Karen needed comforting, even before she became upset.

'If it was anyone else I'd agree with you, but it's not just anyone. It's Veronica. She's one of us,' Karen replies, tears filling her eyes.

CHAPTER SIXTY-FIVE
1976

One of the earliest memories for them all was their very first day of school. Five little kids, four years old, nervous and scared about the new chapter in their lives. Little did they know the things they'd go through together.

Karen was sitting at the table with Jason and Veronica. They weren't talking to one another but they felt comfortable in each other's company. Jason was so full of confidence at the age of four – well, more confident than the rest of them anyway. He flashed Karen a cheeky grin before the teacher guided an upset Jessica over to the table. Her eyes were drowning in tears and her lip quivering.

'You can share Mr Snuggles with me,' Karen told her, holding out her favourite teddy bear.

Jessica shyly took the teddy bear from Karen's hands, although she looked like she was about to burst into tears again at any moment.

'Now then, Veronica, I've got an important job for you. Do you think you can do it?' the teacher asked, crouching down in front of Veronica.

Veronica nodded her head, without muttering a single word. If they'd known then that it'd be the only time they'd get a word in edgeways with Veronica around, they would probably have all been chattering away to anyone who would listen, and even the ones who wouldn't.

'Bradley's feeling a bit shy, so could you look after him for me? You can play together at break time and eat lunch with me. Will you do that for me?' she asked.

'Yes, miss,' Veronica nodded obediently.

'Good girl,' the teacher said.

Bradley sheepishly took the seat beside Veronica and she put her arm protectively around his shoulders before flashing them her mischievous grin, any nerves, any first-day fears disappearing from their bodies.

That was it. Five little children, getting each other through their first day of school. A normal day to everyone else, but to them it was the most special day of their lives: it was the day their friendship started.

CHAPTER SIXTY-SIX
Present Day

Karen paces the floor, each step feeding the anger bubbling inside her. As her six-inch designer heels clash with the cold, black tiles, a ghostly echo fills the room. She despises this place. Instead of unwinding in a warm, cosy home she's greeted each day by a glorified bachelor pad. Not that "His Highness" will ever listen to what Karen has to say. She's strictly for show, just like the Jag parked on the drive, just like this showroom apartment, just like their marriage.

Removing her stilettos, Karen perches on the leather sofa, so enormous it could actually swallow her up. Her hatred for her home and being in Jason's company forces her rage to escape her body.

'Why are you taking Jess's side?' Karen asks, the words flying from her mouth as if her tongue is a venomous snake.

'I'm not,' Jason says, attempting to take her hand.

'Looks that way to me,' Karen snatches her hand away, desperately trying to ignore the goose bumps that lace her skin.

'I'm capable of forming my own opinions. Believe it or not, Karen, I do have a brain in my head.'

'But surprise, surprise, your "opinion" is exactly the same as hers.'

'Because she's right.'

'And the mother of your child.'

'So that's what this is really about,' Jason sighs, pure frustration embedded in his words.

'No. It's about Veronica,' Karen says quickly, feeling her cheeks flush with embarrassment. She shakes her head furiously, trying to regain her composure. 'I couldn't care less about what happened between you and Jess.'

A haunting silence washes over them, Jason's deep brown eyes fixated on Karen's face while she does her best to avoid looking at him. Thinking he's averted his gaze she looks up, only to see that he's still watching her in a way that sends her heart into a flutter. The memories come flooding back.

Their memories.

Karen's thoughts are interrupted by Jason's mobile buzzing noisily, like an annoying fly you can't shake off. She watches him read the text, studying his expression, his mannerisms, trying to work out who it's from. Her mind is racing with questions. Who is it? Is it her? Jess? Why is she texting him? Do they still fancy each other? A tight, nauseating knot forms in the pit of her stomach as she attempts to wrestle the next question from her mind: are they seeing each other again?

Jason's gaze shifts from his phone onto Karen, as if he can hear her insecurities. That's the problem when you meet someone who knows you better than you know yourself: you can never hide anything from them. They know. Whether it be through facial expressions, words or actions, they know how you feel at any given moment.

'It's not from her if that's what you're wondering,' Jason says, dropping his mobile onto the coffee table . . . the bare, unblemished coffee table. Karen prays it won't damage the surface.

Jason seems a little put out by her lack of response, but right at this moment she feels completely consumed with worry.

Karen barely recognises herself anymore, obsessing over muddy shoes and spotless furniture. *Paul made me this way*, she thinks to herself as she looks sadly at her platinum wedding band.

'You're not jealous then?' Jason raises his eyebrows in suspicion.

'Don't even go there,' Karen warns him.

'She's got what you almost had. I understand. It hurts me too,' he admits, crouching down in front of her.

Don't start acting like you care. You've got a kid. Three, in fact. Why would you care about one you never even met?' Karen snaps defensively, fending off the tears she fears may be about to fall.

'She was still here.'

'But she's not anymore. We've both moved on–'

'You shouldn't be with him,' Jason interrupts, his eyes focusing on the red light flashing on the answer machine. Again. Karen hardly notices it anymore. Coming home to the same sight every day, it's almost become like an old friend. She likes it, in a strange sort of way. It brings a bit of colour into an otherwise monochrome space.

'Give it a rest, Jase. What's going on with Veronica is more important than our little domestics,' Karen says, marching into the kitchen, pouring herself a large glass of red wine.

'So you admit he's cheating?'

Karen glares at him, her narrowed eyes a warning for him to go no further with his interrogation. She takes a sip of wine, allowing the liquid to dance around her mouth for a moment before it slides down her throat. The scarlet-red liquor, far warmer than this apartment, eases her racing heart and she takes another sip.

'My opinion hasn't changed. Veronica needs to pay for what she did.'

The coldness of Jason's tone shocks Karen. She can barely comprehend how they came to be this way. As kids they were joined at the hip; never more than a couple of feet away from one another.

'She made a mistake.'

'A mistake is parking on double yellows when you're in a rush, or a kid forgetting their homework. Killing someone is not a mistake.'

'He tried to attack her.'

'So she says.'

'Why would she lie?'

'I haven't got a clue, but it's clear we never really knew her at all.'

'What if it was me? What if I'd killed Mr Carter and gone on the run? Would you say it's all my fault? Would you send me to prison?' Karen asks, throwing questions at him as if she's a police officer interviewing a criminal. No, that's *her* job. Jessica's job. Karen finishes her drink, wanting to drown her jealousy.

'You'd never do something like that.' Jason shakes his head, taking a seat at the kitchen table.

'Did you honestly think Veronica was capable of something like that when we were growing up?'

'No,' he says, bowing his head.

'Exactly,' Karen says.

Karen watches Jason for a while, waiting for a response. He remains quiet, holding his head in his hands, and she can tell he's exhausted with emotion. Fearing she's pushed him too far, Karen joins him at the table, sitting in the seat right beside him.

'Twenty years is a long time, and things are bound to be different, but the change in Veronica is unreal. You saw her. She's an addict, homeless, and without a single penny to her name. She's punished herself more than a copper ever could.' Karen speaks softly, lifting his head up so their eyes lock with each other. 'She's not a villain, Jason. She's our best friend.'

*****

Still taking refuge in the spare room following Jason and Karen's return from Jessica's some time ago, Veronica has pushed her stool a little closer to the door. Having heard everything – Karen fighting her corner, Jason's doubts, the distress in their voices – tears have been rolling down her face for what feels like hours; falling so fast it's like a never-ending fountain. She doesn't deserve their support. Karen shouldn't have offered her this room. She should never have let her bring her back here. She should have kept running.

Veronica *wishes* she'd kept running.

*****

Jason's not sure what to say. He doesn't know what he should say. So he hasn't said anything since their discussion and they've remained in silence. He has to admit it's an awkward silence. For the first time since they first met, all those years ago as little kids, they are sitting in an awkward silence. Even when they split up it wasn't awkward. Just sad.

How could one of their group do such a thing? Veronica, of all people? Of course they got into trouble when they were young, but it was never anything more than a letter home from the school or being grounded for a week. He never thought any of them were actually capable of doing something so cruel. How could she? Was she telling the truth about having to defend herself? Or did she plan it and then think of the sob-story afterwards? Surely, she wouldn't have plotted the whole thing? Not Veronica?

Jason had been so excited when he saw the Facebook advert for the reunion. Finally, after twenty years, he'd see his friends again. Maybe he was foolish to think that they could pick up where they left off, but he didn't think it'd be this difficult: he hasn't been able to catch up with Bradley; Veronica's a changed woman; and then there's him and Karen . . . or rather Karen, Jessica and him.

Karen walks through from the kitchen towards the sofa, where Jason is sitting, and takes the seat beside him.

'You're right,' Karen says, as if she's read his mind.

'What?' Jason asks.

'I am jealous of Jessica. I'm so jealous it actually hurts,' she admits.

'But why? You've got a beautiful daughter of your own,' Jason asks, his gaze falling on the photograph of Amelia. He'd persuaded Karen to take it from the drawer and display it on the side table. Things like that shouldn't be hidden.

'She's not a part of you though, is she?' Karen says, placing her hand under Jason's chin, her soft fingers a comfort against his own unshaven skin. She turns his head so they are looking right into each other's eyes.

'She's better off without me as her father,' Jason tells her. It's the truth. He's been a useless father. He should have taught the boys how to read and write, how to ride their bikes, and helped with homework; instead, his children barely know him.

'Don't say that,' Karen says.

'I've got three children I never see. In fact, I never even knew about one of them,' Jason says.

'You're a good man. You've made mistakes, of course you have, but show me a person who hasn't,' Karen replies, a definite hint of self-loathing in her voice.

'You haven't made many mistakes,' Jason says. He's glad. He'd hate to think of her living her life going from one mistake to another, everything she did resulting in tears and heartbreak. She deserves more. More than him, more than Paul, more than a lonely, clinically cold apartment.

'I've made two and they were the biggest mistakes I could ever have made.'

'And what were they?' Jason asks, unable to take his eyes off of her.

'Marrying Paul,' Karen admits. 'And walking away from you.'

'What are you trying to say, Karen?' Jason asks. He knows what's coming, but he needs to hear her say it anyway. The moment he's been waiting for, for the last twenty years.

Karen doesn't speak, her gaze dropping to the floor. Jason lifts her head so that their eyes lock again, and he gently nods at her, letting her know that she can speak the truth.

'I love you,' Karen says, her voice like a whisper as tears fill her eyes.

'I love you too. I always have,' Jason replies, his emotions mirroring Karen's. He doesn't bother to wipe the tears away. Karen always said she loved his softer side, seeing him being honest about his feelings instead of putting on a brave face like most blokes do. Like she does on a daily basis.

'I'm going to leave Paul. I want to be with you. If you'll have me?' she says, as if she's asking his permission.

'Of course I will,' Jason tells her, unable to believe his luck. He pulls her close, just in case she has a sudden change of heart, but she hugs him back, her arms wrapped so tightly around his body, he feels like she'll never let him go. Jason plants a soft kiss in her hair. 'And we'll take care of Veronica too.'

*****

If any two people deserve a shot at happiness, it's Karen and Jason. Veronica used to be so envious of their relationship back in their school days. But not envious in a bad way. She just used to wish she could meet someone who made her feel the way they made each other feel. She could never manage it though. Never short of attention, she used to play on it, flirting with anyone that offered her a smile, blagging free drinks for her friends. It's no wonder she always ended up bringing trouble to the door. She didn't mean it though.

She didn't mean any of it.

*****

It feels like Jason's in a dream. Or just back in time. Sitting here on the sofa with Karen, his feet propped up on the coffee table with Karen's head resting on his lap. It doesn't last long though, as they are interrupted by the clatter of keys in the door.

'Is that . . .?' Jason asks, his heart suddenly beating faster – although he doesn't know whether it's fear or excitement.

'He said he wouldn't be home tonight,' Karen says, jumping up from the sofa.

'Maybe his mistresses were busy,' Jason says.

'Of all the nights he could turn up unannounced, he chooses tonight,' Karen says, breathless with panic. For a moment, just a moment, she was at ease. She was happy. Now she's back to square one.

There's no time to tidy up before Paul stalks into the apartment, like a proud lion returning from a day's hunting. As the smug grin dissolves from his face in a matter of seconds at seeing the state of his "show home", Jason can't help but smile. He deserves everything he'll get.

'Well, I've had better welcomes,' Paul says, running his eyes over the apartment, cups and dishes on the side, Jason's shoes by the sofa. 'I see you've made this place your own while I've been gone.'

CHAPTER SIXTY-SEVEN
Present Day

Watching as Bradley wearily pulls his coat over his body, Jessica can't help but feel guilty. It's crazy really. She's completely innocent. She's the one who gets rid of people like Veronica. Yet here she is feeling guilty when she's off God knows where, probably thinking she's got away with it, yet again.

'Will you be okay to drive home?' Jessica asks him.

'I'll be fine,' Bradley says, sounding as though he is completely drained of energy, and yet he must now go and break some truly devastating news to his wife.

'I'm sorry that I had to tell you about what Veronica did,' Jessica says.

'You did the right thing,' he tells her.

'What are you going to tell Danielle?'

'The truth. It's what she's been waiting for.'

'I can't even begin to imagine how messed up she's been,' Jessica says, instantly regretting her words. The last thing she wants to do is upset him anymore. 'Sorry, that's probably not the right word, but . . .'

'No, you're right. She has been a mess. To be honest, there have been times over these past few years when I thought we were over. She gets so paranoid, so stressed out. It's been a difficult time,' he replies.

'You're a good man for standing by her,' Jessica says.

'It's a husband's duty, isn't it? For better for worse and all that,' Bradley says, exhausted.

'I wouldn't know. I've never quite got that far.'

'I really should get back to her actually. She'll be worried.'

Bradley lingers for a moment, wishing he didn't have to go home and face his wife. Although it is the information they've been waiting for, the information that will help get them back on track, it won't be easy for him breaking such terrible news to Danielle.

'Keep in touch, won't you?' Jessica says, and without muttering another word, Bradley leaves.

CHAPTER SIXTY-EIGHT
Present Day

Paul works his way round the room, tidying everything away, desperate to have his show home back. Firstly he takes the wine glasses from the side, putting them on the kitchen counter; then he moves Jason's shoes, smirking as he does so. They're not like his smart, designer black shoes, they're scruffy white trainers. He throws them in the box beside the front door before he turns his attention to the photo sat on the side table: Amelia.

Karen's blood boils watching Paul carry out his uptight routine. Even though she doesn't love him, she still wants him to fight for her, get angry, demand an explanation; instead, he's acting completely normal, as if there's nothing to fight for, as if he expects Karen to fall to her knees at any moment, in floods of tears, begging him for forgiveness.

Paul takes hold of the photo, looking at it for a few moments before putting back in the drawer, out of sight. Then he turns to look at Karen, a big grin on his face. A smug grin, like he's done her a favour. He makes her skin crawl.

'Are you gonna stand there all night or are you gonna come over here and give me a kiss?' Paul asks, holding out his arms.

'No,' Karen tells him.

'No?' Paul asks, a frown etched on his forehead.

'We're over, Paul. Me and you,' Karen says.

'Over? How can we be over?' he asks, completely floored by what she's told him. She's standing up to him for the first time in years.

'It's simple really. I want a divorce,' Karen tells him firmly.

'You're making a big mistake,' Paul says through gritted teeth. 'Where do you think you'd be without me? Who do you think you'd be?'

'I'd be happy and that's good enough for me.'

'You're happy now. Look at everything I've given you. Most women would kill for a home like this. A husband like me.'

'Think a lot of yourself, don't you?' Jason says, but Paul ignores him.

'I haven't been happy for years, Paul, and if you were any sort of husband, you'd have realised that,' Karen says.

'And you're gonna be so much better off on your own, are you?' Paul asks, mocking his wife.

'I won't be on my own,' Karen says.

Paul pauses for a moment, a little confused, before he looks at Jason, who now has one arm round Karen's shoulders. Karen watches as the penny finally drops for him, and she has to admit, she likes the feeling. He can be the one left all alone for a change. He can be made to look the fool.

'Oh, I get it. This is your new bloke, is it? The one you're leaving me for?' Paul asks, looking Jason up and down, judging him.

Paul edges closer and closer to them, his glare fixed firmly on Jason.

'You like this place, do you? You think that by getting into her knickers, you're gonna get your hands on this apartment, that fancy motor on the driveway outside? Well, you can think again. You're getting nothing,' he tells him.

'I don't want anything. I love Karen,' Jason says.

'*Love*?' Paul asks, as if Jason is speaking another language.

'Yeah. I know it's something you can't understand. Men like you don't know the meaning of the word,' Jason replies.

'Jason, leave it. He's not worth it,' Karen says, not wanting him to get involved.

'Jason?' Paul says, turning his attention back to Karen, a face like thunder. 'Is this the bloke you kept banging on about when we first got together? What did you call him? Your "childhood sweetheart"? Have you been having an affair with him all along?'

'No.'

'Liar!' he shouts, his voice bellowing, getting right up in Karen's face. He always does this. But this time it won't work. He won't break her down.

'Don't talk to her like that!' Jason says furiously, pushing Paul away from Karen. 'Is it any wonder she wants out of your marriage when you treat her like this?'

'You'll be nothing without me,' he says, still glaring at Karen.

'She doesn't need you,' Jason tells him.

'Who do you think paid for that car on the drive? Who shelled out the cash for that stupid salon of hers? Eh? Me, that's who!' Paul says.

Seeing him screaming at Jason is the final straw, and a red mist clouds Karen's vision. She feels her hands begin to shake as she opens her Prada handbag. She finds the two sets of keys and shoves them at Paul. Stood right in front of her husband, she gets a whiff of perfume. Not £100-a-bottle perfume like she has on the shelf in the bathroom. Cheap perfume. There's a faint pink mark on the collar of his shirt too. A familiar sight after one of his "business trips".

Karen opens his hand, shoving one set of keys into it so hard she thinks they'll leave an indent in his palm.

'The keys for the car,' Karen says, before placing another set of keys into his hand. His greedy hands. 'The keys for the salon. Go on, take them!'

'Once I take them, you'll never get them back,' he tells her as if he's expecting her to change her mind.

'I never wanted all this stuff in the first place.'

'Women would kill to be in your shoes.'

'So you keep saying,' Karen says, rolling her eyes. She used to be desperate to impress him, but now she can't stand him.

'It's true,' Paul replies.

'The only thing that's true is the way I feel about Jason,' Karen tells him, slipping her hand into Jason's. This time she's not letting go.

'You loved me once,' Paul says.

'I did, yeah. But not in the same way. I loved you because you could keep me safe, because you were strong and ambitious. I was lonely when I met you. If I'd have known then that I'd be more lonely in our marriage than out of it, then I never would have gone through with the wedding.'

CHAPTER SIXTY-NINE
Present Day

The TV is on but Jessica doesn't know what she's watching. She's not really taking it in. It's some mind-numbing documentary on a subject she has no interest in. The people on the screen are talking but she can't hear them. She's been unable to concentrate on anything since Bradley left. At least when he was here she had a distraction, someone to talk to, but now it's just her alone in this room, her mind is going into overdrive.

Why did she do it? How did she do it? Why didn't she confess before? Why did I have to find out?

Jessica's thoughts are interrupted by the sound of Natalie coming out of her bedroom. She turns the TV off and takes a deep breath, preparing for the row that will inevitably start.

'Mum?' Natalie says quietly, walking towards Jessica, the arm of the sofa in between the two of them, acting as a barrier.

'Finally speaking to me then?' Jessica asks.

'I shouldn't have gone off like that. You've got enough to deal with. So, you know, I'm . . .' Natalie mutters, her voice trailing off.

'Sorry?' Jessica says, finishing her sentence. A smile creeps onto her lips as she watches her daughter shuffle from one foot to another. 'It's a five-letter word, Natalie. It's not that hard to say. Why don't you give it a try?'

'I'm sorry,' she says. It's no exaggeration to say Natalie has never really apologised for anything in her life, so this takes Jessica by surprise – although it's a very welcome surprise.

'I'm sorry too,' Jessica says.

'For what?' Natalie asks, sitting on the sofa, now removing any kind of barrier between herself and her mother.

'For not telling you who your dad was,' Jessica replies.

'I never really asked though, did I?' she says.

'You shouldn't have to. It's every kid's right to know their parents,' Jessica says, feeling guilty.

'I understand why you couldn't.'.

Jessica's shocked. It's like Natalie's had a personality transplant overnight and she rests her hand on the teenager's forehead, a little smirk creeping onto her lips.

'What are you doing?' Natalie asks, a little confused.

'Checking to see if you're coming down with something. Only, the daughter I know would never have a mature, civil conversation with me,' Jessica asks.

'I do now,' Natalie tells her.

'You sure you don't want to slam a door or stomp your feet?' Jessica asks, making Natalie giggle.

'I guess I'm growing up,' Natalie says, shrugging her shoulders.

'I guess you are,' Jessica says, smiling at her. For the first time in a really long time, she feels proud to say Natalie's her daughter. 'So, does this brand-new Natalie stretch to a cuddle for her mum?'

Jessica holds out her arms and Natalie immediately falls into her embrace, hugging her tightly. It feels nice. She hasn't hugged Jessica for years. In fact it's been so long, Jessica can't actually fully remember the last time they were like this.

'I was wondering . . .' Natalie says, interrupting the quiet, as if a little nervous. 'Can . . . I see my dad?'

*****

It's been a couple of hours since Veronica heard Paul enter the apartment. Scared that he'd barge into the room, she'd propped herself against the door as best she could, careful not to make too much noise. She's pretty sure Karen hasn't bothered telling him that she's staying, and one look at Veronica, a scruffy no-hoper in his smart, shiny apartment, would have sent him into panic mode.

There's a knock at the bedroom door and Veronica cautiously opens it, to be greeted by Karen and Jason standing a short distance away.

'Is everything alright? I didn't think I should come out of the room before. I didn't want to cause problems for you . . .' Veronica says. She's aware she's rambling on, but the looks on Karen and Jason's faces tell her there's reason to worry.

'We're going to have to move you,' Karen tells her.

'Where to?' Veronica asks, her heart filling with dread once more.

'Jason's flat. We can't stay here anymore. Paul will be back at some point and he's not exactly going to be understanding, is he?' Karen replies.

Despite trying her best to remain unfazed by the latest turn of events, Veronica can tell it's beginning to take its toll on Karen, each breath is short and fast, and she has a panicked look in her eyes.

'I should go. I never should have dragged you into all this,' Veronica says, shaking her head. Now they're back together, they deserve to have a happy life, a proper family. She won't get in the way of that.

'We don't have to protect you–' Karen says.

'So don't. Let me leave,' Veronica says, interrupting her, desperate to stop them getting themselves into trouble.

'We don't have to protect you, but we want to, because you're our friend,' Karen replies.

'Jess is supposed to be a friend too. And Bradley,' Veronica says.

'They've shown where their loyalties lie,' Jason says.

'And I haven't been friends with Jess for a long time, so there's no real loss there,' Karen shrugs, having finally given up on a reunion with her former best friend. 'It's just the three of us from here on in.'

*****

Making her way towards the front door, Jessica's heart is in her mouth. She wishes, more than anything, that she didn't have to do this but there's no other way. No-one will ever take her seriously if she doesn't. Why would they? She needs to use her career to help the Carter family. After twenty years, they deserve to put their demons to rest and have the chance to grieve properly.

'Where are you going?' Natalie asks, poking her head round her bedroom door.

'I need to go to the station,' Jessica replies, grabbing her coat and leaving the flat before she has the chance to change her mind.

CHAPTER SEVENTY
Present Day

Just as Jason and Karen guide Veronica into the lift, ready to move her safely over to Jason's flat until they figure out a better plan, Jason's mobile buzzes in his pocket. He immediately looks at the notification: a text from Jessica. Karen watches his face drop.

'What?' Karen asks, her eyes wide with terror.

'We need to pick up our pace,' Jason says.

'Why? What did the text say? Who's it from?' Karen asks.

'Jess,' Jason says, holding out his phone so Karen can read the message: *Last chance to get Veronica to safety.*

'What? What did it say? Show me,' Veronica says, having been shielded from the message.

'It's going to be fine. Just trust us,' Jason says, wanting to offer her reassurance. He puts his phone back into his pocket and checks his watch, beads of sweat emerging on his forehead.

Karen tries her best to remain calm, but the prospect of their friend being caught and thrown into prison terrifies her. She's desperate for the lift to go down to the ground floor faster.

*****

No sooner have Karen and Jason got Veronica out of the apartment building than they hear sirens, so high-pitched it feels like they could burst their eardrums. A haze of blue flashing lights fills their vision and, before they know it, police cars surround them, the tyres squealing as they screech to a halt. It's like a scene from an action movie. Only it's not a film. It's real. Jessica has set them up, having sent the warning message when she and her colleagues were already halfway there, so they'd know they'd catch Veronica before she was moved on.

'I need to g-go,' Veronica says, her throat closing up, causing her to choke on her own words.

She tries to pull away from Karen, but she's clinging onto her too tightly, and she isn't strong enough. Jessica, now dressed in full police uniform, climbs out of her car, heading straight for them.

'Jess, don't do this,' Karen begs, trying to keep her grip on Veronica, but Jessica forces them apart.

'You've been running from this too long. It's time you got what you deserve,' Jessica says to Veronica, taking out a pair of handcuffs and slapping them across her wrists, covering the daisy chain tattoo. 'Veronica James, I'm arresting you for the murder of Brian Carter–'

'Please don't do this to me,' Veronica says, tears filling her eyes. This is it. Her life over. She's facing life in prison. One split second decision twenty years ago and it's ended her life.

'You do not have to say anything but–' Jessica says.

'I'll never step foot out here again. I didn't mean to do it! I'm sorry. Please!' Veronica cries, tears streaming down her face, her legs weak, unable to believe that the thing she has been running from all these years has actually happened: she's been caught.

'But anything you do say may be given in evidence on which you later rely on in court,' Jessica continues, showing no emotion towards Veronica.

Veronica is so distraught that her body is close to giving up, her voice only allowing two words to escape her lips: 'My son.'

As Veronica is led over to a police car, Karen collapses to the ground, falling onto her knees, letting out the most gut-wrenching cry, devastated that she's not been able to save her friend. Jason, as ever, is at her side, trying to remain composed for Karen's sake, even though his heart has also been shattered into a million pieces.

ONE YEAR LATER
CHAPTER SEVENTY-ONE
Bradley

A piercing cry wakes me from my sleep and for a moment or two, my heart races with panic, the noise reminding me of the events of last year: the deafening sirens, the heart-broken screams that had been caught on camera and shown on the news report; but then I remember, this sound isn't something to fear. It's the sound of my future.

Climbing out of bed, being careful not to wake Danielle who is sleeping peacefully despite the noise, I throw my dressing gown around me, the soft, fluffy fabric a comfort at this time of day, shielding my skin from the early morning chill, and I tiptoe towards the door. The hinges creak, reminding me of the endless list of household jobs I'm still to complete. It's getting longer by the day, but since our world was turned upside down two months ago, there doesn't seem to be enough hours in the day.

I turn my head to check I haven't disturbed my wife. She deserves a lie in. After all, it's not often I am here to take the burden, thanks to my ever-demanding job. She needs to make the most of it, take it easy. She stirs a little but she soon settles back down, her eyes staying closed. A year ago, she would wake in a cold sweat after a nightmare and it'd sometimes take hours to calm her enough to sleep again. The sweet smile on her lips is a welcome sight and one I hope will not disappear any time soon.

Making my way towards the room opposite ours, my eyes run over the sign on the door: Bryony. A tribute to her late grandfather, Brian Carter. It was always something Danielle wanted, to make her father a grandparent whether he would meet the child or not, so when that day came, I suggested honouring our daughter with his name. There will always be questions over whether Veronica had acted in self-defence, whether Brian had mistreated her . . . but of course Danielle would never even consider it to be true. It was just a relief to finally have justice and to be able to rebuild her life.

Going into the nursery, painted a shade of pink similar to the living room and bedroom, I immediately make my way towards the pristine white cot stood in the corner – the cot that carries my princess. I pick up my precious bundle of joy, snuggling her close to my chest. It's often the only way I can get her to stop crying in the morning, like the closer she is to her father, the safer she feels. I hope so, anyway.

Within a few minutes, Bryony has settled into a slumber once again, only letting out the occasional whimper. I'm sure she only does this because she wants to be the centre of attention at all times, making as much noise as she can to notify us of her presence – something she's certainly inherited from her mother. She's beautiful like her mother, too, with thick dark lashes that rest delicately on her soft skin as she sleeps, and pink lips that naturally form into a small pout.

I feel two arms wrap round my waist and hug my body tightly, a head rest against the top of my back. I don't have to turn around to know it's Danielle. Her sweet fragrance fills the room and as I turn my head to the side slightly, I get a whiff of her hair, smelling the coconut shampoo she loves so much.

'I love you,' Danielle whispers, her voice making my heart melt. There was a time, about a year ago, when I feared we wouldn't make it. I was convinced we were heading for the divorce courts. But then the truth about Veronica came out and, despite it being one of the hardest days of my life, it was also the turning point for me and my wife, the day her demons were laid to rest and we could finally concentrate on being a proper couple and, now, a proper family.

CHAPTER SEVENTY-TWO
Jessica

'Congratulations, Sergeant Palmer,' my boss says, handing me my police badge. It's the first time for as long as I can remember that he actually sounds happy to have me as part of the team. I haven't let him down by letting my temper rule my head. I've worked hard and made him proud.

"Sergeant Palmer". I've been waiting a long time to hear those words. Months, years, of relentless work have at last paid off. My bravery has finally been rewarded. I think of Darren, all the times he belittled me, hurt me, made me feel like the smallest, least important person in the world. Success really is the sweetest revenge.

Sergeant Palmer. It sounds so good. It feels good. Until I look at the small photo on my new badge. A more recent, modern photo of myself, taken only a few weeks ago . . . but instead of making me smile, it haunts me.

I remember the day so clearly, as though it was yesterday. Dragging my body, weighed down with shock from my flat, along the pavement to where my best friend was sobbing, in a heap on the cold ground. I'd been crying too, something that ignited my anger as I wiped the tears from my face, my make-up smeared across my hand, the black mascara tarnishing the skin.

You should never cry on the job. Never. We're not there to show weakness or get too involved. We're police officers. We show up, solve the crime, and move on.

Who was I kidding? The events that unfolded that day weren't scenes from a Hollywood blockbuster. They weren't pieces of puzzle. They were real life. Veronica was my friend and we were outside my flat. This was a day in my life. My friends were my life.

It was in that moment I realised I needed to come clean. I'd spent the week pretending to be someone else: a hotel cleaner on minimum wage. I was, in fact, a police officer. I had been an officer for seven years prior to that day, desperately working towards some kind of promotion, but always getting overlooked . . . yet I'd lied to my friends when they had asked.

I knew that if I told them what my job was when we'd first met up, they'd start treating me differently. That's what people normally do. They're happy to have a laugh and crack jokes with you until they realise you're a copper. You can even pinpoint the moment their mood changes. The smiles fades, like a light switching off, and they swallow, clearly feeling a little nervous, despite the fact they had been doing nothing wrong. I wanted my friends to treat me like the Jessica Harper they knew twenty years ago, not DC Palmer.

My hands were shuddering uncontrollably as I reached into the back pocket of my jeans. I couldn't stop them, no matter how much I tried. I've never been very good with shock. Mind you, who would be good at finding out that their friend, someone they'd known since they were four years old, was a murderer?

I don't think Karen and Jason will ever forgive me for getting Veronica sent down; but what was I supposed to do? Despite her being a close friend, she'd still committed a crime, and if anyone else did what she had done, they'd be sent to prison too. Doesn't stop me feeling guilty though. Standing here, having been awarded a promotion, knowing Veronica is a year into her life sentence.

I love my job. I always have. It gives me a purpose, lets me help people. The heart-wrenching sadness when a call comes in about a murder or a missing person to the pure elation of seeing justice being done. I get such a buzz from it, slapping handcuffs on the wrists of criminals and carting them off down to the station.

I just never thought I'd have to arrest one of my own.

CHAPTER SEVENTY-THREE
Jason

People always say it's the little things that mean the most. When I was a young lad, I didn't believe it. How can something small, something that costs no money, make me happy? It's impossible. I needed a flash car and a posh house, all the luxuries you could ever dream of. Or at least I thought I did. Then I had Karen on my arm and my whole perception changed.

We used to sit up all night, just talking and laughing, not a care in the world. Or we'd walk through the park and share a picnic with the others. We didn't need expensive holidays and posh dinner dates. All we ever needed was each other, and if I hadn't have been so stupid all those years ago, we would have carried on that way . . . but that's all in the past now.

Going downstairs I've never felt happier. My place of work has changed. Instead of a rundown bar just off the High Street, I'm now the proud landlord of a much-loved pub. When I took this place on nearly a year ago, it was a hollow shell – perhaps not literally, but there was no sense of life here, just an empty building. Now it's warm and welcoming; a place that brings in a steady stream of regulars each night of the week. This pub is something I can be really proud of; something I can build up to pass on to my children.

That's something else that's changed. My family. Behind the bar is a photograph of my pride and joy. Go back a year and I wasn't allowed to see my twin boys, but now they come to stay every weekend. I've got a good relationship with

Natalie too – a surprise considering Jessica wants nothing to do with me.

We've been joined by Amelia too. After Karen's divorce from Paul, we took Amelia out of boarding school and enrolled her in a place not too far from our pub. Both she and Karen seem much happier, much more bonded, being under the same roof. She's taken to me really well, and the boys and Natalie. When they're all under this roof, it's like they've always been around each other, like they grew up together. Soon we'll be a proper family and I'll become not just a father and a husband, but a step-father too.

I whisked Karen off to Paris after Veronica was arrested. She was devastated, having witnessed that, and I wanted to do something to help. Paris might seem like the standard option, predictable even, but it made Karen smile and that's all that mattered to me. When we reunited at the party, I knew that I never wanted to let Karen out of my sight again and so, while we were taking in the sights from the Eifel Tower, I got down on one knee and asked her to be my wife.

We're getting married in two months. Nothing too extravagant, just a small wedding with family. We've sent an invite to Bradley, in the hope that we could reunite once again, forget all the bad things that we said and move on, but we've yet to receive a response. I won't lie, I'll be gutted if he's a no-show on my wedding day, but like Karen always tells me, the most important people will be with us. Our children. The boys. Natalie and Amelia. Our family.

CHAPTER SEVENTY-FOUR
Karen

If Jess and Bradley knew where I was right now, they'd say I'd got a screw loose. Not that they'll ever find out. The day Veronica was arrested was the day our friendship ended. Again. Only this time I don't think a reunion will be on the cards. I made a choice and that choice was to support Veronica. It cost me a lot, not financially, but emotionally. They think it was easy for me to side with Veronica, that I never really cared about them in the first place, but they couldn't be further from the truth. It broke my heart to walk away from them. I blink hard as tears sting my eyes.

Sitting at this table in the middle of the room, I feel so uncomfortable. Until the age of forty-one I'd never set foot in a prison, and I never thought I'd have to. But here I am, now forty-two, sat in the visiting room, the same way I do every week. Well, almost the same.

A hand reaches out and rests on my back, obviously sensing my nerves. The hand belongs to a young man I barely know. I should be supporting him, not the other way around. This could be the biggest, most scary moment of his life, but instead of wallowing in his own feelings, he's looking after me. I'm grateful. My nerves are shot; my heart thumping so hard, I'm sure it'll burst out of my chest.

Then I see her walking towards us. Or rather hobbling towards us. She's not had an easy time since being in prison. It's not the first time I've come to visit to find that she's been the victim of a beating. Her left eye is swollen, almost bulging out of its socket, her cheek a mix of deep purple and yellow, and there's a cut on her mouth, dried blood staining her lips. Hardly surprising, given her crime, but my heart goes out to her all the same.

People used to stare at her when we were teenagers. We'd be in a club and the crowd of people would part, as if a celebrity had just arrived. She was beautiful, bright and funny, perhaps even a little wild at times, and everyone loved her for it. She was never bullied at school, never had any enemies. It was impossible to hate Veronica and, for the four of us, it was impossible to ever stay mad at her. She'd flash you her cheeky grin and even if you didn't want to, you'd find yourself grinning back.

That cheeky smile is nowhere to be seen as she makes her way towards the table. I haven't seen it for well over a year, since the day I washed and dried her hair for her. Her pace is slow, very slow, and I can see she's in great pain.

As she gets closer to the table, I can see her expression change. It's no longer one of hurt. Instead a bewildered look inhabits her face. I hadn't told her of my plans, wanting it to be a surprise, and I hope that it will have the desired effect. I find my right hand finding its way to my left, twirling my diamond engagement ring around my finger. I'm getting my happy ending and, despite what others might think, Veronica deserves hers too.

CHAPTER SEVENTY-FIVE
Veronica

I can't breathe. This can't be real. Each week I come out of my cell to find myself being greeted by Karen and, on occasion, Jason. Today there's someone else sat beside Karen.

Karen stands up, talking to me as she does so. Or at least I think she's talking to me. Her mouth is moving but I'm unable to take in any sound. I nod at her, letting her know I'm okay, and she offers a soft smile before leaving the room.

My legs feel like jelly as I struggle to stay standing. My knees buckle then and I'm on the floor. The ground is cold and I fall with a fair amount of force, but it's like my body is numb and I can barely feel a thing. A hand appears in my peripheral vision and as I turn my head, in what feels like slow-motion, I see Jayden. Or at least that's what I called him twenty-one years ago. He could go by a different name now. One thing's for sure, he looks just like me. He has my eyes.

Jayden helps me up from the ground, despite a passing security guard glaring at us. He says something to the guard, prompting him to walk away, and turns his attention back to me, offering me a kind smile. I'm still in shock. My heart pounding with such force I feel as though it's about to burst through my chest. He seems like a caring, respectable young man; the type of man any mother would be proud of.

'Hello, Mum.'

Two words I never thought I'd hear fill my ears and I can't hold my emotions inside anymore. As he embraces me, I exhale, causing my tears to flow from my eyes like a waterfall.

It's the moment I've always dreamt of, although not in this particular circumstance, and I can't believe someone has gone to so much trouble to bring me such joy. It's far more than I deserve and, in this moment, I know I owe a lot to Karen.

The only good thing that's ever come from me. My boy. My son.